D0495225

C334770876

PRAISE FOR *TASTING SUNLIGHT*

Over 400,000 copies sold in Germany
THREE YEARS on the German Bestseller List

'A stupendous debut. A triumph. Don't miss it' Louisa Treger

'It reminds me of those books that shaped me as a younger reader ... books written for the pleasure of language and character, without a glossy high-concept premise or a big twist. It's a sensory joy; a novel of quiet, understated beauty that gives its secrets away slowly, but is no less compelling for that. Original, luminous and intense, it's a mesmerising read' Iona Gray

'A truly special book. Powerful, lyrical and profoundly affecting, Ewald Arenz spins a tale of friendship, restoration and possibility with utmost heart and care. I loved it!' Miranda Dickinson

'Written with beautiful simplicity, this sensitive and profound story examines how we heal and help each other, delivered with deep insight and huge heart' Doug Johnstone

'It reminded me of reading Sally Rooney's *Normal People*. It takes a writer of immeasurable talent to make you feel that intensely, merely by evoking ripening late-summer fruit and the sound of rain on dusty ground' Elizabeth Haynes

'Powerful, original and engaging. I loved it' Susie Boyt

'Nothing and yet everything happens in this story. The simple minutiae of everyday life becomes intricate and essential: rituals that connect one woman to the land and her heritage, and show a lost, younger one a different truth. Moving, heart-wrenching but ultimately uplifting' Carol Lovekin

'An exquisitely written, heart-warming story of two damaged women who form an unlikely friendship against the backdrop of a farm. The smells, tastes, sounds and rhythms of nature are described with sensuous clarity, so you feel as if you are there, picking potatoes from the earth, tending the bees, and tasting the pears. Just beautiful!' Gill Paul

'Sometimes less is more. *Tasting Sunlight* is breathtakingly beautiful' Louise Beech

'Poignantly, gently and profoundly evocative' TripFiction

'A very special story that will leave no one untouched ... the author's love of nature shines through' *Bilt*

'Ewald Arenz has, in the most exquisite way possible, showed how two wounded souls can heal one another ... a triumph' *Nurnberger Zeitung*

'Raw and tender, brutal and gentle, striking and perceptive all at once' *Doppelpunkt*

'It's rare for a friendship between women to be written with such enchanting, impressive honesty. And by a man. Bravo!' *Stadtmagazine*

'A simply wonderful, heartwarming read' Fiona Sharp, Bookseller

'One of my top reads of 2022. I absolutely loved this book – the beauty of the writing, the complexity of the characters ... a story that breaks your heart, and fills it too' Bookly Matters

'The perfect story for our time. It is uplifting and healing ... Truly exceptional, a novel with heart and with characters and a setting that are alluring, beautifully created and totally enchanting' Anne Cater

'It's a special, beautiful novel that is timely and needed' Café Thinking

'A book full of empathy. This beautiful book is written without shallowness or trite answers and it touched my soul' Live & Deadly

'A beautifully crafted novel which will stay with me for a long while' Sally Boocock

'Absolutely cracked me open and put me back together again' Jenn Morgans

ABOUT THE AUTHOR

Ewald Arenz was born in Nuremberg in 1965, studied English and American literature and history and now works as a teacher at a grammar school. His novels and plays have received numerous awards. *Tasting Sunlight* was shortlisted for the German Independent Booksellers' Favourite Novel of 2019 and was on the *Spiegel* bestseller lists both as a hardback and paperback. Ewald lives with his family near Fürth.

Follow Ewald on Twitter @EwaldArenz and his website: ewald-arenz.de.

ABOUT THE TRANSLATOR

Rachel Ward is a freelance translator of literary and creative texts from German and French to English. Having studied modern languages at the University of East Anglia, she went on to complete UEA's MA in Literary Translation. Her published translations include *Traitor* by Gudrun Pausewang and *Red Rage* by Brigitte Blobel, and she is a member of the Institute of Translation and Interpreting. She has previously translated Simone Buccholz's *Blue Night, Beton Rouge, Mexico Street* and *Hotel Cartagena* for Orenda Books.

Follow Rachel on Twitter @FwdTranslations.

Tasting Sunlight

EWALD ARENZ

Translated by Rachel Ward

ORENDA
BOOKS

Orenda Books
16 Carson Road
West Dulwich
London SE21 8HU
www.orendabooks.co.uk

First published in German by DuMont 2019
This edition published in the United Kingdom by Orenda Books 2022

A catalogue record for this book is available from the British Library.

ISBN 978-1-914585-14-2
eISBN 978-1-914585-15-9

Typeset in Garamond by typesetter.org.uk
Printed and bound by CPI Group (UK) Ltd, Croydon CR0 4YY

The translation of this work was supported by a grant from the Goethe-Institut London

For sales and distribution, please contact info@orendabooks or visit www.orendabooks.co.uk.

Tasting Sunlight

1 September

At the top of the ridge, the air was shimmering over the asphalt. To Liss, as she drove the old, open-top tractor slowly up the narrow lane through the fields and vineyards, it looked like water that was more liquid than ordinary water; lighter and more agile. You could drink it only with your eyes.

The fields glinted with stubble after the harvest, yet the wheat was still present in the overwhelming scent of straw; dusty, yellow, sated. The maize was starting to dry, and the rustle of it in the gentle summer breeze no longer sounded green; it was turning hoarse and whispery around the edges.

The afternoon was hot and the sky was high, but when you switched off the engine, you could suddenly hear that there were fewer bird voices now and that the chirping of the crickets had grown louder. Liss could see and smell and hear that the summer was coming to its end.

It was a good feeling.

Nobody was running after her. Nobody was following her. Nobody had got into a car to drive slowly down the country lanes along which she'd been walking for two hours now, climbing steadily for the last forty-five minutes. And, frankly, why should they? It wasn't like she had to report in somewhere on the hour. Although, she'd had that experience.

Sally stopped and turned around. The crappy countryside lay spread out beneath her in the sun. Ten thousand fields with whatever in them, while far off on the horizon, dim in a hazy summer smog, lay the city with the clinic on its outskirts. Such a lovely, leafy location. With an avenue. A proper tree-lined avenue, right up to the gate. The avenue had been kind of important to Mama. As if the trees were some sort of guarantee that she'd be especially well looked after there.

She sat in the grass at the edge of the farm track. It wasn't a proper road, just concrete slabs, each of which was precisely eight and a half steps long. She'd counted the steps because it was important not to step on the cracks. And now she sat down on the side of the road, pulled up her knees and wrapped her arms around them. It was hot. She'd hitched a few kilometres, but the guy who'd picked her up had been an idiot arsehole. He'd gone on at her the whole time. One question after another, plus you could hear the ones he wasn't asking out loud: Where've you come from? What's your name? What are you doing? Are you going home? Still the summer holidays? Am I a stupid, moronic arsehole? Do I pick up hitchhiking girls because I think I'm the caring, sharing type, when really I just want to drive them somewhere for a quick shag? What's your name then? Spit it out.

At some point she'd just reached for the handbrake and pulled it up. And got out. She didn't need that shit. Not today. Not ever, actually. And anyway, it was better to walk. Climb the hill, even though it was so fucking hot.

Fucking hot. Fucking hot. Sally repeated the phrase to herself, just to hear her own voice, which had dried out in the hot air. She pulled her water bottle from her rucksack. It was almost empty. There was a scattering of apple trees across the slope beside her, with masses of apples that might have quenched her thirst, but she wasn't falling for that. Eating wasn't a thing today. It really wasn't. She hated having to eat when other people said so, or because it was just the thing to do. To eat because it was morning. Or midday. Or evening. Or because you were hungry. She wanted to eat when she wanted to eat. She wanted to drink when she wanted to drink. Nobody understood that.

She took the last two swigs of the lukewarm water and screwed the lid back on the empty bottle. At the top of the hill was a village. She was sure she'd be able to fill it up there somewhere. And if she couldn't, she couldn't.

She got to her feet to carry on up the slope. It wasn't late yet. Once she'd put the village behind her, she'd be able to look out for somewhere to sleep. It was still warm and she had ... It was only now that Sally realised she'd never slept in the open air. In a tent, sure; back in the day, they'd gone to the same campsite in Italy year after year. With ten thousand other families who were all spending Whitsun in Italy too. What great parents she had – so imaginative. On the other hand ... sleeping in the open air was probably another of those things that sounded more romantic than it actually was. You'd most likely get ants crawling in your ears and up your nose. And then there were ticks. Maybe she'd find a barn or something.

The farm track came out onto the village high street, which was much steeper than she'd expected and ran past a few farm houses for one or two hundred metres or so to the main road. Ten minutes later, she was finally at the top, and she stopped for a moment to get her bearings. The village wasn't very big; from where she was standing, it was only a few steps to the edge of the place. She could see a long way over the countryside. There were wind turbines standing in loose ranks in the fields; their blades turned unhurriedly in a late-summer wind that she could barely feel from down here on the ground. Thank God for the wind turbines. Everything was so fucking idyllic, it was all she could do not to scream. She longed to crouch down and piss all over the middle of the road. Just to make something dirty.

She should have headed back to the city centre. But it was always crawling with police. And she didn't feel like being around anyone she knew. She hadn't felt like being around people she knew for ages.

Just before the village sign, she passed a front garden where a lawn sprinkler was throwing tired jets of water over the flowerbeds. Without looking around, Sally climbed over the fence, pulled the hose off the sprinkler and filled her bottle. When it was full, she drank a few more swigs straight from the hose, threw it onto the lawn and jumped back over the fence onto the road.

Liss had uncoupled the trailer because you couldn't turn the tractor on the narrow path between the vines with it hitched to the back. It was more practical to unhook it and manoeuvre it around by hand. But as she'd turned it round, one of the front wheels had slipped into the gully between the track and the field, and now the drawbar was at such an awkward angle between the vines, she couldn't get the tractor close enough to hitch it back on and pull the trailer free. The wheel was slotted perfectly into the gully, and that meant she couldn't shift the shaft any further. The trailer wasn't too big for her to move it on a flat road, but she'd need more than just physical strength to get it out of the gully. Suddenly, she didn't know why, she found herself thinking about Sonny. About the young Sonny from the old days, not the other one. He'd liked this kind of thing because he took such pleasure in his own strength. If something like this had happened, to the camper perhaps, he'd have jumped down into the ditch and braced himself against the van; she'd have put her foot down a bit until it got free again, Sonny pushing with all his strength.

Free.

Liss heard the word echoing in her head and straightened up, blinked involuntarily then looked down. The shadows of the vine leaves were sharp, their edges clearly defined against the pale concrete of the path, but blue around the edges. When she looked up again, she had to shield her eyes from the now slanting sun. It was a wide landscape. The river lay like a belt, glittering as far as the eye could see. She was free, she told herself. She could go wherever she liked. She gave the stuck trailer another tug, pulled with all her might. Then she saw the girl coming up the farm track.

Sally didn't notice the woman until she straightened up. Tall. Slim. Wearing a blue ... what was that? A work dress? It looked a bit like those overall things ... what were they called? Like a boiler suit. A boiler dress. And she was wearing a headscarf too. Countryside clothes. Super fashionable.

Really, she'd have preferred to dodge through the vines to avoid her, but that would've looked kind of weird, because the woman had now seen her. Sally walked a little faster when she realised the woman was looking at her. And in such an odd way. Not curious. Just ... the way you might study an animal – a beetle running over the road. One of the ones that shimmered in that gorgeous shade of green-gold but were actually dung beetles. Because that was how things were: if it looked like gold, it lived off shit. She squeezed past the trailer that was slung diagonally across the path and, despite herself, lowered her head a little as she walked past the woman.

'Can you just grab hold of this a moment?'

The question was so unexpected that Sally jumped. Yet it had been asked perfectly calmly, like a genuine request, without making any demands. It wasn't hiding an order like such questions normally did. 'Would you give me a hand?' 'Would you like a bite to eat?' Would you pass me the water, please?' The type of shitty question where the honest answer was: No. I wouldn't like to. I'm only doing this because you're stronger than me. Because you have all the say. Because, for whatever reason, you can make me do things. But: No! I don't want to. Don't even ask me. Don't act like I have a choice. Just issue commands. Say: Sally, you little shit, help me. Sally, I can't stand you, I hate you and your parents because I'm working in this crappy clinic earning half what your father earns, but I get to make you eat. Sally, Sally, Sally, Sally, Sally, pass me the fucking water, you little bitch. But none of you dare say that.

'Can you just grab hold of this a moment?'

It was a genuine question. A question that could be answered with a 'yes' or a 'no'. She had stopped, but now she turned around and looked at the tall woman. And the trailer with one of its wheels stuck in the ditch.

'Yes,' she said. 'Shall I push?'

The woman eyed her briefly, but she didn't say that Sally was too thin, too skinny. She didn't use any of the words that the others used in order to avoid saying what they meant.

'Are you strong?' she enquired calmly.

Another question Sally hadn't been expecting. Nobody had ever asked her that before. In her whole amazing, awesome, wonderful life. What kind of woman was this?

'Kinda.'

'OK, then you keep pulling the drawbar round to the left. I'll try to rock it out.'

The woman had gone behind the trailer and leant her back against the trailer's tailgate before she noticed that nothing was happening up at the front. She turned to Sally and, after briefly giving her another of those funny looks, she pointed to the forked piece of metal with a hole in it.

'That's the drawbar.'

Then she turned away again, braced her back against the trailer and began to rock. Sally picked up the drawbar. After a while she started to feel the rhythm and could pull when the woman pushed, push when she let go. The wheel was rocking ever more violently up and down the walls of the ditch, and then, all of a sudden, the trailer came free and Sally had to stumble forward to stop herself falling.

The woman had her hands firmly on the tailgate and was keeping the trailer on the road. She was smiling almost imperceptibly.

'Thanks.'

Sally nodded.

'Can you drive a tractor?' the woman asked. Sally, instantly furious at the stupidity of the question, turned on her.

'Do I look like I can drive a tractor?' she snapped. 'Do I look like I've got a driving licence? Do I fucking look eighteen?'

The woman had stopped smiling and was looking at her again, as if her gaze came from the sea or across the mountains; at any rate from somewhere miles away.

'That isn't what I asked,' she replied, as matter-of-fact as if they had been real questions; and calm, unreproachful, 'but it doesn't matter. Could you get me two stones and put them under the front wheels? Not too small, please.'

Sally hesitated. This woman wasn't giving off that social-worker calm that they all had in the clinic. She wasn't wearing that none-of-this-fazes-me face that they all put on if you yelled at them or insulted them, or just said nothing. That face that you longed to spit in.

She walked to the ditch and looked around. There were lumps of stone everywhere, as if someone had piled them there on the edge. OK, someone probably had. Picked them out of the vineyard to get them out of the way. She chose one: triangular, like a wedge, dusty white, warm from the sun. The broken edges felt good, almost sharp. She pushed the stone under the first wheel, while the woman stood patiently holding the trailer and looking at her. Sally hurried with the next stone.

'OK?' she asked.

The tall woman took her hands off the tailgate.

'OK,' she answered. 'Thanks.'

She walked over to her tractor, reached into the engine and pressed something. Sally heard the engine turn over, incredibly slowly. Like an old man taking his first few steps after waking up, hesitant, as if he were about to fall. It sounded as though someone needed to give the tractor a pat on the back. But then the motor picked up speed and suddenly it was ticking along evenly. The woman got aboard and reversed the tractor so skilfully that the drawbar was almost touching the coupler. Sally found herself reaching for the shaft and lifting it.

'Bit further,' she shouted over the noise of the diesel engine. The woman let the tractor roll ten centimetres further back and the drawbar hitched itself up. Sally saw the small iron rod that hung on a thin chain from the coupler, took it and shoved it through the lugs. She looked up to the woman on the tractor, who'd turned in her seat to face her and was now putting her thumb up.

'The locking pin too,' she called.

Sally bent and saw the little pin that had to be shoved through a small hole in the bar to stop it slipping out of the drawbar. It looked a bit like a clumsy hairgrip. She stuck it through and then stepped back onto the path between the trailer and tractor. The tractor jerked, the woman raised her hand as if in farewell, and Sally picked up her rucksack again. A little dust whirled up as the tractor chugged its way further uphill between the vines. Sally followed slowly. There were grapes on the vines. Much smaller than the ones she knew from home. Dark blue with a white film. She picked one and popped it in her mouth. One would be OK, but definitely not ... It wasn't properly sweet. You could taste that it wasn't ripe, but it wasn't like an unripe apple. The flavour was already there. She spat out the skin and walked on. She didn't notice for a while that the tractor had stopped again, a couple of hundred metres ahead. She heard the engine running and saw the woman on the seat. What did she want? She walked a little faster, wondering again if she should walk through the vineyard, go cross-country, but then she felt annoyed with herself. What was this about? The woman didn't even know her. When she passed the idling tractor, she saw that the woman had rolled a cigarette. She half turned to Sally and said, just loud enough to be heard over the engine:

'If you like, you can stay on my farm.'

Sally's first impulse was to act like she hadn't heard her. How did she know she wasn't walking home? Her second was to run away. She looked up at the tractor. The woman had struck a match and was lighting the cigarette. Only after that did she glance down at Sally again.

Stuff it, thought Sally. Stuff it. She threw her rucksack into the trailer, climbed on one of the tyres and swung herself over the tail lift. She didn't sit with the woman on the tractor. From here, she could always jump down again.

The woman took her foot off the brake and breathed out smoke. The tractor coughed out smoke. Sally sat on the bottom of the trailer, her back to them both, pulled up her legs and watched as the village behind her grew fuzzy in the shimmering air and then disappeared. It'd be great to dissolve like that, she thought, vanish into hot air and light.

2 September

It was just before half past ten when Sally emerged from the room Liss had given her and walked into the kitchen. Nothing special. Sink, cupboards, fridge – furniture you'd forget the moment you left the room, Sally thought. But where there had once been a window onto the farmyard, there was now a glass patio door. It was ajar. A bright strip of sunlight lay slanting across the tiled floor. Standing on the table were a plate, a cup and a covered bowl. A teapot beside them. Everything looked clean and tidy. Sally sat down on the bench along the wall, from where you could see through the door out into the yard. She took the plate off the bowl. Small pieces of fruit. Apple. Pear. Kiwi. A few nuts mixed in. And honey. You could smell it. Hesitantly, she covered the bowl again and touched the teapot with the back of her hand. It was lukewarm. Sally poured herself a cup. To her relief, it was black tea. Why was one of the fundamental principles of every bloody clinic in the world that they only ever had a load of herbal teas? Everything always smelt of camomile and peppermint. Even if you got hold of other teabags from somewhere, the tea would still taste of camomile and peppermint. The taste wormed its way in everywhere. The clinic crockery was so steeped in it, whatever you brewed automatically turned into peppermint or camomile tea.

She found herself laughing at the idea, and almost jumped because it was such an unfamiliar sound.

She took the plate off the bowl again, fished out a piece of pear with her fingers and popped it into her mouth. It tasted sweet and had a mild spice that Sally didn't recognise. She wondered whether it was in the pear, or whether Liss had spiced the fruit salad. She took a piece of apple. It tasted completely different, so she tried the pear again. Perhaps it was just that she hadn't eaten since yesterday morning, but the pear tasted special. She picked out a walnut. That simply tasted of walnut and honey. Sally drank a sip of lukewarm tea. She liked the way the bitterness first mingled with the taste of honey and then turned clear and tart in her mouth. Hastily, she covered the bowl again and stood up. She took the cup with her as she stepped through the French window into the yard. The tractor was gone, but the trailer was standing half in and half out of the barn door, just where they'd uncoupled it yesterday. Sally wandered across the yard. She hadn't been able to look around yesterday. Liss had shown her where she could sleep – it wasn't until they were standing in the spartan room that she'd told Sally her name. Sally hadn't answered and only later, when she'd come back down into the kitchen, had she introduced herself to Liss in return. Liss had nodded, but not with the satisfaction that other adults so often showed, which left no doubt that they'd been waiting for her finally to come to her senses, finally to see that she'd done, acted, been wrong, for her finally to cave give in come crawling back. That nod that was always like hoisting a flag, like a trumpet proclaiming victory. The nod that was meant to look understanding and yet always hid a very slow whiplash.

Sally set one foot on the drawbar and drank another sip of tea. Liss was funny. She'd never met anyone like her. What kind of woman was she? The house was far too big for her, but Sally had sensed immediately that she lived alone here. You could tell whether or not a house was lived in. And this house was big and empty. The room she'd slept in hadn't been used for a long time.

Sally did a lap of the barn. It was so beautifully dark on this bright September morning. A row of agricultural machines stood there in the dim light; she hardly recognised any of them. What did Liss do? Was she a farmer? What was she doing on her own on such a big farm? Sally looked up. Above her, light shimmered through the cracks in the wooden ceiling. There were no steps up to the hayloft, only a ladder. She put the cup down on one of the machines and climbed up. As she rose through the hatch, she saw to her surprise how much brighter it was up here. There were glass tiles in the roof, at regular intervals. Only the gable walls had proper windows. Perhaps it was down to the clear September day and the height of the sun, but the huge loft looked friendly and quiet. The dust fell so slowly through the beams of sunlight that it seemed almost to stand still. You had to look very closely to notice that it was falling, incessantly falling. There was a large heap of hay across the back third of the loft. Cords were hanging from the beams and above the hatch was a large wooden wheel, running over which was another rope, its long end lying in large coils beside the hatch. It was a good place. For the first time in a long time, everything within Sally fell perfectly quiet, and she stood still so as not to immediately lose that quietness again. She watched the dust in the light and felt the same way: as if she were falling very slowly; so slowly that there was no need to fear the impact.

A while later, she climbed down again, picked up her cup and roamed across the farmyard, past the empty stable, along the path into the garden, past a hen house, past round woodpiles among which the hens were pecking, past an ancient privy that was leaning against an empty rabbit hutch. The garden itself was more of an elongated meadow – as large as a field. Part of it was fenced in and laid out for vegetables. Sally wondered at first why you'd put up a fence in your own garden, but then she remembered the hens. Opposite the vegetable garden was a low, windowless building with wide sliding doors. Sally pulled at one and saw that it was a machine shed. There was a second ancient tractor, a plough and a few other pieces of equipment whose function was equally mysterious; there was a pile of sacks, and then there was a motorbike. Curious, she walked over. She'd ridden a motorbike once, illegally, of course. Sally swung herself onto the seat and tried the kick starter. The engine didn't start. She tried it again, and, now becoming absorbed in what she was doing, kicked down once more on the starter. Nothing happened. She kicked it until a cramp shot down her calf and she had to jump up to stretch her leg. Furiously, she kicked at the motorbike; it fell over. What was she doing here anyway? What kind of insane game was she playing here?

She ran out of the building, down the path out of the garden and into the yard, ran through the kitchen into the house, then up the stairs into the room she'd slept in. She grabbed the rucksack from the chair, felt automatically for her phone, remembering almost simultaneously where she'd left it: jammed behind the back of her wardrobe in the clinic. Switched off. According to her phone, she was still there. She pulled a face. She was free. Nobody knew where she was. She could go wherever she wanted. She threw on the rucksack and went down the stairs. In the kitchen, she stopped. Wonderful. The question now was, where did she actually want to go?

'Away isn't a direction, huh?' she asked aloud. The door was open. The kitchen was empty. The strip of sunlight had flitted past the table and was now lying kind of in the doorway. The sun was at its noonday height, and its light was leaving the room. For the sun, things were simple.

It reminded Sally of a kindergarten rhyme and she sang it tunelessly: 'The sun is rising in the east and heading south for now at least before it goes down in the west yet northern climes are not so blest.' She'd hated kindergarten.

In the end it didn't matter where she went. It wasn't about getting anywhere. It was about getting away from everything.

As she pulled the patio door shut from the outside, she remembered the cup. She'd left it by the motorbike in the equipment shed. Somehow it felt wrong to leave without putting the cup back in the kitchen. She walked down the path past the woodpiles. The hens ran around between her feet as if she weren't a stranger. In the machine shed she looked around for the cup. She'd set it precariously on the tractor's dusty, green mudguard. But before she reached for it, she took a few quick steps towards the overturned motorbike and picked it up. Then she hastily took the cup and ran out of the shed down the path.

Liss was just turning into the farmyard on the tractor when Sally reached it; she jumped lightly down from the seat and reached into the engine to turn it off. It chugged to a stop. Smiling, Liss looked at her.

'You're leaving?' she asked with a glance at the rucksack.

Sally shook her head and raised the cup.

'I was just in the garden,' she mumbled, and walked into the kitchen.

3 September

It was raining. For the first time in weeks. Good for the wine. As Liss pushed the courtyard door open into the dawn, the air, cool and grey, streamed into the kitchen, which was still warm, almost a little sticky with the warmth of summer. She drank her tea standing, leaning against the doorframe. It was a steady pouring rain. There were puddles in the yard. The hens ran from the stable to the barn and back. That was a life, and who was to say it was wrong, just because it looked pointless from a human perspective?

The girl was still asleep. She was sleeping in the room Liss had given her as if it were her own. Liss walked over to the stove and poured herself more tea. Then she leant against the doorframe again and watched the rain. A day when you ought to just leave the world to drink and not bother it. When you ought to just let the hens run without shaking your head over them. A day when you ought to let a sleeping girl sleep. There was a reason for everything, she just couldn't see it.

Liss stepped back into the kitchen, laid the table and then fetched her waterproofs. She was about to go when she looked back at the table and hesitated briefly, before eventually fetching a piece of dark bread from the larder and laying it beside the bowl of fruit. Then she went out into the rain and exhaled deeply as the first cool drops fell onto her face.

It hadn't been raining then. But it had sounded like it. It had been thawing. Those days in February were the saddest ever. The icicles on the gutters melted and dripped ceaselessly onto the lead roofs of the hen houses, the rabbit hutches, the woodshed. The sky seemed to have no flavour. The puddles in the unpaved yard were up to her ankles. The fences by the road were still buried, metres deep, beneath the dirty, hard snowdrifts, a whole winter's worth, and you couldn't imagine that it would ever be summer again. She'd been doing her schoolwork and staring longingly out of the window. Now she was outside on this quiet Saturday afternoon, and it felt as though she were entirely alone in the village. Everyone else could have been dead or have suddenly vanished. She could hear nothing but the steady dripping and, now and then, the heavy soughing as a load of snow on one of the roofs started to slip, then drummed down onto the yard. She imagined actually being entirely alone. The village was as extinct as the aftermath of a nuclear war in one of the futuristic novels she borrowed from the local library and read when her father wasn't at home. He didn't like her reading. She left the farm and walked down Haselau lane, the heroine of a sci-fi novel. The village looked black and white amid the spent snow, like something out of an old film. In the bakery she could see Anni, tidying up the display. The woman gave her a pretzel every morning as she stood with the others outside the shop window, waiting for the bus. Now she was beckoning her in, but she couldn't go, because she was on a mission and Anni was nothing but a flickering image on one last television running on the last of the electricity in a plundered shop in a deserted city. She walked further down the narrow street, past the Berger farm, past the parsonage garden wall, on which she sometimes lay face down in the summer, her whole body absorbing the heat of the sun-sated stones. Those were special afternoons, and only very rare. When she'd crept away with a book that she then couldn't read, because as she read, the images sharpened and, if she squinted a little, the air above the parsonage roof gradually turned as blue as a southern sea. When she and the wall she was lying on had travelled away, unnoticed, into a small, hot town by the sea, and she was no longer Elisabeth but Zora, and no longer had any parents, but was free to go wherever she wanted. And shimmering over the rooftops was the sea.

She hunched her shoulders. On a February day like this, it was a certainty that she'd never see the sea; worse still, it wasn't even certain that there'd ever be another summer day when she could dream, at least for an hour and a half, of being somebody else.

Hey, Elisabeth!

Thomas.

My name's not Thomas anymore. I'm called Sonny now. Are you coming?

Thomas was odd. Everyone in the village knew that his father was a bit too free with his fists. But he still kept laughing.

What are you doing?

Come and see. I'll show you.

He ran ahead, fast, kept turning back to see if she was following. At the last farm – which she didn't know at all because no child ever went there, not even to say their thank-yous at Carnival when you got a mark, or even two, at every house – Thomas ran round the back into the garden.

Look.

Proudly, as if he'd built it himself: a huge concrete basin. At first she thought it was for slurry, but when she leant over the wall she could see that it was perfectly clean. At the bottom was water, maybe a metre deep, floating on which were proper, thick ice floes, as large as tabletops. Thomas was already swinging himself over the wall, holding a stick that he'd taken from one of the woodpiles.

Come on.

She only hesitated briefly. Then she fetched herself a stick too, lay on the wall on her belly and let herself down onto the ice. And was surprised that it held. Cautiously, she pushed herself away from the concrete wall with the stick and drifted slowly over to the other side. Thomas laughed. They grew braver. Their laughter echoed in the concrete basin. They lurched and jumped from one icesheet to another, pushing each other away. And then Thomas tried to push her off the ice with his stick.

Stop that!

You try. Let's see who's stronger.

Stop it! I mustn't go home wet.

Thomas stabbed at her with the stick. She had to brace herself against the wall and pushed her way into the middle, veering between laughter and anger.

Your father's got the biggest farm in the village. He can buy you new clothes.

She pushed his ice floe away. He wobbled, had to drop to his knees to avoid falling.

Has not.

She didn't even know whether theirs was the biggest farm. She'd never thought about it.

Thomas had got up and kicked hard at the edge of her ice sheet. She lost her balance, slipped, and then she was standing up to her hips in the ice-cold water. To her surprise, she could feel a delay before the icy water ran into her boots. Thomas seemed far more shocked than she was.

I didn't mean to.

He was whispering.

Help me out.

She was furious.

It was only then that she noticed that they had to be standing on the ice to reach the wall again. Suddenly, there was the fear.

Help me!

But Thomas had already hopped up, was trying to reach the

coping at the top of the wall. She was battling the ice. The sheet kept tipping, breaking, because they were both moving so wildly, with such fear, and was consequently getting smaller.

Help me!

Thomas had reached the coping and pulled himself up.

I'll get a stick.

He was gone. Impelled by rage and fear, she hurled herself onto an icesheet with a single, furious leap, lay there until she'd calmed down, and then stood up cautiously. Her legs were trembling. She pushed herself against the wall and jumped with shaky knees, gripped the edge, pulled herself up. Her trousers were heavy with water, but she managed it. She saw Thomas standing on the log pile. He still hadn't found a long stick, but he was laughing again.

Think it's funny, do you?

Jerk.

She ran home without looking back for him. But that evening, in bed, she thought back to punting on the ice, and it was only then that she understood why Thomas had laughed. After all, it wasn't an adventure if it wasn't dangerous. Properly dangerous, not like in a book. From outside she could hear the steady drip of the melting icicles, and she fell asleep with the thought that the ice floes would be shrinking now too.

5 September

It was Friday, and still nobody had found Sally and had a long, gentle conversation with her, unreproachful, sympathetic, with hatred concealed behind every gentle word. Hatred for her because she wouldn't fall into line, because she kept running away and because she didn't listen to their soft, sympathetic, empathetic voices, but kept looking them in the eye, until the fake wall of professional niceness and warmth and understanding crumbled, and she could see the boredom and uninterest and hatred shining behind it.

It was Friday, and still nobody had found her.

She lay in bed in the bare room, which lacked all the things they always thought she needed to put her at her ease: there were no pastel colours and no tasteful pictures on the wall, no friendly wallpaper and no cuddly carpet that you always longed to puke over from the moment you first walked in. It was just a room with white limewashed walls; there was no carpet, there was only one chair, which wobbled a bit, and there were no curtains at the window. It was a room like clear water, and it felt good to lie there. Yesterday it had rained, and she'd stayed in the house almost all day. In the morning, she'd listened to the sounds that Liss made in the kitchen and the bathroom. She'd gone downstairs once it had gone quiet, and had found tea again, and the covered bowl of fruit. There was bread on the table too, and a saucer of butter. No challenge. Just an offer that looked as though Liss had seen the bowl of fruit untouched the day before and thought that maybe Sally preferred bread. Sally put the butter away in the fridge, which wasn't in the kitchen but in the little pantry with its sloping ceiling, which followed the staircase above. She'd looked into the bowl to see if there was pear in there again, and she'd eaten every bit of it, plus two or three walnuts. She'd taken the tea upstairs with her and sat at the window, and spent the whole day looking at the yard, at the road outside the farm, and the bakery on the little village square across the road. She'd watched the people buying bread. Some stood outside the shop to chat, despite the rain. She'd watched the hens, which came down to the yard from the garden over the course of the day; there, they searched for earthworms in the narrow, uncobbled strip by the fence along the road. She'd watched Liss, who, wearing her yellow waterproofs, had driven her tractor into the yard around noon, and then vanished into the barn for hours and come out again with very dirty hands, without looking up at her even for a second. She'd drunk coffee with Liss, when she'd come to the door and called that there was coffee. They hadn't talked. Then Liss had stood up again and walked out, and Sally had put the coffee pot on the stove and rinsed out the cups. Later she'd been upstairs again, had been on the bed, reading a book she'd found; after that she must have fallen asleep, even before it had got dark, because now it was Friday.

It was Friday, and nobody had found her.

She stood up and walked to the open window. It was still very early, but it was going to be sunny. After the rain yesterday, a fine mist hung over the farm.

The farm. Why did the woman live here all alone but then let people live with her? Images from films about psychos briefly flickered in her head. Lonely farm. Mist. Forest. A garden full of dead girls. She grinned the pictures away. The place she'd come from *was* full of dead girls, but they didn't realise it, so they just kept moving. Zombies.

Anyway, the woman wasn't like that. But what was she like? Not so easy to pin down, somehow ... Maybe it was easier to say what she wasn't: a witch. A psychopath. A social-worker-trust-me-bitch. There weren't that many people who really trusted you. Without constantly saying so, to make them believe it themselves. Strange. She was definitely that. Strange. In a kind of cool way, but strange, all the same. Sally thought hard, but she really didn't know anybody who actually lived alone. Let alone in such a big house.

♠

There was a knock on the door. Sally turned, expecting the door to open before she'd said 'come in' because that's how it always was. But Liss actually waited. Sally walked to the door and opened it.

'Good morning,' said Liss. She was wearing a blue linen headscarf, which framed her face in an odd way. Sally resisted finding it attractive.

'I need to harvest potatoes today. Can you help me?'

'Right now?' she asked.

'I can easily wait till you're ready. There's always plenty to do on the farm,' Liss answered with that little smile that Sally had got to know by now.

'I'll come,' she said.

♠

This time, she sat with Liss on the tractor. There was a seat over each of the large back wheels; on one side you could sit on planks of wood, long worn smooth and polished to a shine, but on the other there was just the bare metal of the mudguard. Running around both seats was a steel tube that served as both backrest and handhold. Sally could feel every jolt. They drove through the village out onto the lane. The vineyards dropped away on their right. She could see far over the valley, where the morning mist still hung over the distant villages while it was already bright sunshine up here. To their left were fields up to the forest, perhaps a kilometre and a half away. They turned onto a side track. The thing Liss had hitched to the tractor jolted and clattered along behind them. A potato spinner, she'd explained as she'd pulled it out of the shed in the garden. Not that that explained much. The track led in a slight curve along a hedge, and then they suddenly stopped. To their right was a field. Liss took a jute sack from the pile under her seat and threw it onto the edge of the field. She gave Sally an iron basket. Then she climbed down onto the drawbar and released a lever. The spinner sank. It looked like a kind of plough, but behind it was a wheel with slightly curved prongs sticking out of it at intervals – a bit like the round broom on a street-sweeper truck.

'How do you know when the potatoes are ready?' asked Sally.

Liss jumped off the drawbar and pointed at the ridge.

'Go on, dig one up.'

Sally crouched in the furrow and dug her finger into the soil under the potato plant. It was warm and still a little damp from yesterday's rain. When was the last time she'd dug in the ground? When was the last time she'd had her hands in the earth? She couldn't remember.

'Here,' she said, when she hit the potatoes and unearthed them.

There were eight or nine tubers of varying sizes. She brushed off the earth and looked at them. They were pale, almost glowing in the September sun.

'Give one a good rub,' Liss commanded.

'And?' asked Sally, once she'd rubbed a potato completely clean.

'If the skin doesn't come off, they're ready. Or you can dig some up and cook them to see if they're OK, but that'll take too long just now.'

Sally looked up in surprise. It was the first time Liss had made a joke.

'Collect the potatoes in the basket first and then put them in the sacks,' Liss said, already sitting in the seat again. 'Don't lug them any further once they get heavy, I'll chuck the sacks down to you at intervals. And take your time.'

Then she put her foot down and the wheel started turning. Now Sally saw what the plough bit was for. It lifted the earth out of the ridge, the broom flung it aside, and the potatoes spun out with it. It looked a bit ridiculous, unprofessional, almost gawky. But as she slowly walked along the furrows behind the tractor, she could see that it worked. You just had to pick the potatoes up.

You just had to pick the potatoes up! After the first two hours, Sally's back hurt so much that she wasn't even bending anymore, just shuffling along on her haunches. Liss had long finished with the spinner and was gathering them up too. Sally watched her as she came up from the other end of the field, in the other furrow, moving like a machine. Bend. Gather. Shove the iron bucket along a metre. Bend. Gather. Empty the iron bucket into a sack. She was much faster than Sally; she noticed that because with every furrow, Liss met her further along. And they hadn't even done a third of the field.

'Stuff this!' she screamed, suddenly furious. 'Just stuff this.'

She hurled the potatoes she'd just picked up across the field, but her arms hurt so much it looked a little ridiculous. They only flew a few metres. Sally straightened up. What was this? Some kind of work as therapy? Did Liss think she'd fall for this shit? She was allowed to stay with her, so she had to play along and pick up potatoes to heal herself through healthy country labour? Was that it? She looked for Liss. She was about seventy metres further down. Bend. Pick. Potatoes in the basket.

'No,' said Sally angrily. 'No. You can all do one. You can all do one, you arseholes.'

She walked to the nearest sack, almost full, and tried to push it over. That wasn't so easy. It only fell slowly, and the potatoes barely rolled out. Sally bent and ripped the two bottom edges; grabbed a potato in each hand through the rough jute and bellowed wordlessly with rage, while tearing at the sack with all her strength, then suddenly fell over backwards as it emptied far too quickly. Panting, she lay there a few seconds before, still burning with rage, jumping up and running to the edge of the field, past the tractor that Liss had parked there and then sprinting, as fast as she could, for the forest.

Liss watched the girl go. Instinctively, she'd jumped up, wanting to call after her, but then she just stood and watched her go. You can't run away from work, her father had told her coldly once, when she'd been meant to be raking up the scraps of hay behind the trailer. It was the most boring job in the world. The hay cart ahead of you in the field, always a step faster than you could rake. The monotonous, metallic sound of the scraper that pushed the hay back once the tines had caught it. All the sounds were monotonous, they wove a net of grey thread in which she was caught, in which she was dragged along behind the cart, having to rake up the ridiculous scraps of hay that hadn't been gathered up. How much had it been, she thought, and for a moment the hatred rose up within her with its bitter taste; a wheelbarrow's worth perhaps? Or two?

At some point she'd just stopped. The cart rolled on, and she'd stopped. How old had she been then? Thirteen? Fourteen? She couldn't remember. She'd watched the rake tip over. The tines lay pointing up. Good. And then she'd gone into the wood. The sounds clung to her like threads. The chug of the motor. The excruciating little scraping sound of the iron crossbar on the floor of the cart. The dreadful, repetitive screech of metal on metal from the hay spindle beneath the truck. She'd walked into the forest until she couldn't hear any of it anymore. When she'd come home hungry in the late afternoon, he'd locked up the kitchen. And the pantry. Even the cellar.

Those who don't work, don't eat.

Sometimes she'd have preferred it if he'd boxed her ears. Or shouted. But he didn't do that. No shouting. No laughing. No nothing.

You can't run away from work. Those who don't work, don't eat.

She'd found herself unripe apples. Tomatoes from the garden. She'd fought for two days, soundlessly, stubbornly. Locked kitchen. Locked pantry. Locked cellar. Where there weren't invisible threads, there were locks. Eventually, she'd climbed on the tractor, thrown the wheelbarrow into the trailer and driven to the forest meadow to rake up the hay. And she'd imagined setting fire to it in the winter, the hay in the barn, and him standing down below and not noticing, and then the floor burning through and falling on him.

Liss took a deep breath.

Run, girl, she thought.

Then she bent down to the nearest potato.

It was dark by the time Sally came back. It was quiet in the village, but not silent. Now and then a car drove by. As she passed the sheds, the cows' chains clanked. They couldn't run away, Sally thought, they always stood there. Blue light flickered behind a lot of the windows. The people were watching TV, she thought with tired scorn, they were sitting in their cramped houses, really believing that they'd been transported far away, had escaped, when actually they were sitting in their living rooms, chained up, staring at a wall, just like their cows.

Her legs hurt. She'd walked a very long way, had kept forcing herself on until she'd got into the zone walking always brought. But it had worn off eventually, and now everything hurt. Her legs from walking. Her arms and back from picking potatoes. And something inside her that always hurt, yet which she didn't always notice.

When she reached the farm, she stopped. There was still a light on in the kitchen. Had she chained herself up too? She was tired. And she felt hunger, which she could normally push away, but she was too tired even for that. The air was still warm. A cloud of midges buzzed around the lamppost outside the entrance. Sally leant against the fence and looked into the farmyard. The tractor stood there. The potato spinner had been swapped for the trailer, on which stood the sacks of potatoes. She could hear a quiet, sleepy clucking from the hen house. The patio door into the kitchen was open a crack. So what, she thought, so what. She shook herself and walked across the yard into the kitchen. There was a plate at her place. A saucer of butter. A little cup of salt. And a black enamelled pan. Sally stood by the table, too exhausted to resist. She lifted the lid off the pan. Potatoes. Boiled in their skins. They were still lukewarm. Sally stared at them. Then she took one out, broke it open and dipped one end cautiously in the salt. It tasted like coming home, and suddenly her eyes welled with tears. She ate another. With the skin and a tiny dab of butter. And then another, just with salt again. She put the lid quietly back on the pan, switched off the light and put the butter in the pantry. Then she went up to her room.

6 September

Liss stood in the kitchen and looked at the table. The pan was still standing there but the butter had been put away. The knife had been used, the plate hadn't. She lifted the lid and looked in. Then she carried the pan into the cool larder. As she put it down, she stopped for a moment. They used to do their own butchery on the farm. The heavy beechwood butchering bench was still in the pantry; long, dark and worked smooth. Hanging over it were the boning knives, slim and sharp; cords for tying up sausages; a meat cleaver that you could see had been sharpened again and again over the decades. All things that had once had a purpose but which now, in their forgottenness, looked nice but were no longer useful.

Some people were like that too.

She was like that.

The girl, by contrast, could still find a way into the world.

A piece of matt, grey September sky shone dully through the tiny window; the wall was almost a metre thick at that point, where the brickwork bulged over the cellar steps. She looked into the pan again. Yes. There were fewer than yesterday. Liss stood there in silence. Then she put the lid back on the pan without a sound. Most people no longer worked with the earth, from which everything came. Most people had forgotten that things could grow in autumn too, and that you had to be more careful with them than with the things that came shooting out of the ground in spring.

What about you? she thought through the ceiling, up to where the girl lay. What about you? It was still less than a week since the girl had thrown her rucksack into the trailer and climbed up over the tyres. It seemed longer. For someone who is always in one place, six days are nothing. One day is like another, and they flow into one another. For someone on the run, six days are a lot. The girl was making her days lengthen and no longer fly past so unnoticed.

Liss looked at the knives. Sharp. Thin. Some were only fit for a particular butchery task and were otherwise never touched.

Some people were probably like that too.

She was like that.

7 September

Sally was now waking up a little earlier each day. In fact, the days were getting shorter, but somehow it didn't feel like that here. When she got dressed, she realised that she needed to do some laundry. She'd run out of underwear. And her jeans weren't exactly fresh. She walked over to the little window, which stood ajar, and pushed it right open. It was a little overcast but not cold. She could easily wear her shorts. It looked like the sun would come out properly later on. She threw on her hoodie and walked down to the kitchen. Sally was surprised to see Liss eating breakfast at the kitchen table. It was the first time they'd seen each other in the morning. She was reading the newspaper and drinking tea, taking these little, regular sips, as if her mind wasn't really on it and she was actually somewhere else. Sally had often noticed that about her. Liss looked up amicably and said good morning. Sally mumbled something along the same lines and sat in the spot on the bench where she'd been sitting the last few days. She felt a bit awkward with Liss there.

'Tea?' asked Liss, reaching for the pot. Sally nodded and pushed her cup slightly towards the middle of the table. Liss poured for her. As Sally took back her cup, she noticed Liss's glance fall on her thigh, and catch there for a moment before she turned back to her newspaper. Sally took a deep breath. She knew that look.

'What?' she asked aggressively. 'What?'

Liss laid the paper down on the table.

'I was looking at your legs,' she answered frankly.

'Yes, I saw,' Sally spat, but less furiously than she'd have liked. She'd been expecting the usual 'nothing'. Now she looked at her own thighs. On the insides, the scars lay side by side like tallies. It didn't look so bad, she thought. A tally chart. Shit day shit day Ben Ben Ben Ben shit day Mama shit day clinic clinic Ben Papa Eve shit day sixteenth birthday shit day. That was her left thigh. That was where she'd started. She'd already forgotten a few of the marks. That was good. Because really it was an inverted chart. The scars wiped out the days and the faces and the feelings.

She took a gulp of tea. Whatever. Let her look.

Two tallies on the chart on her right thigh were still a little red. That was kind of fitting too. They started off red and eventually they faded to an inconspicuous pale. And the days they stood for faded with them.

Let her look.

Liss pushed the newspaper over to her.

'They're looking for you.'

Whenever she got a proper shock, it felt like someone inside her throwing cold water at the walls of her stomach. And her mouth was suddenly dry. She took the paper and read the brief report. Missing person ... Sally ... blah blah age ... blah blah height ... therapeutic centre in W— ... information to...

Sally read the report again. And again. Of course. What had she been thinking? That she could really just disappear? That they'd really leave her in peace? Arseholes. The lot of them.

'Maybe you should text someone. Or email.'

Liss had put one foot up on her seat and was hugging her long leg as she looked at Sally.

'I ... I lost my phone,' Sally said, far too loudly. 'And I don't want to message anyone.'

There was a long silence. Liss drank tea. Then she stood up, walked past Sally and opened the door to the yard.

'Do you want to go or stay?' she asked without turning back to Sally.

'I want them to leave me in peace. I wish they'd just leave me in peace.'

Now Liss did turn around.

'Then you ought to give them a chance to do that,' she advised in the calm voice that Sally normally found kind of awesome. 'Write and tell them you want to be left in peace.'

'Yeah right.' Sally leapt up. The teacup fell over. The tea flooded onto the newspaper. 'Yeah right! Why d'you reckon I lost ... I threw my phone away? I don't want anyone to find me. I want to be left in peace. Why doesn't anyone get that?' She was almost screaming now. 'I want them just to leave me in peace and not keep on and keep on and keep on mucking me around and going on at me and wanting to figure out stuff that isn't even there. I want to be dead to them. They don't need to know I'm alive. They're all such fucking arseholes and...'

Liss suddenly smiled. That wound Sally up even further, but Liss interrupted her.

'Nobody has to know where you are. The advantage of a letter is that it doesn't involve signals or phone masts and you can post it wherever you like.'

Sally gave her a long stare. What did she want? Why was she doing this?

'Write a letter,' repeated Liss, without pushing it. 'If you succeed in playing dead, it'll have unpleasant consequences in that people will start to think you really are dead. And that'll make everyone uptight. And I don't want uptight people on my farm.'

Sally used the newspaper to mop up the tea so that Liss wouldn't see that she ... that she was surprised. It was the most Liss had ever said.

'Aren't you...' She didn't know how to phrase the question so that it didn't sound silly. 'Do you have a problem with me staying here?' she finally blurted, in the voice her teachers – who just didn't get a thing – had always called rude.

'No,' answered Liss. She turned brusquely away and began to clear the table. She left the bowl of fruit. As ever. Sally watched her. Liss put the cups in the sink and half turned to Sally.

'I have to go into the forest today. Tagging. Want to come?'

Sally nodded, even though she didn't know what tagging was, and took a piece of pear from the bowl.

'Why do your pears always taste of spice?' she asked.

'Do they?' Liss asked in return, a little surprised. She took a piece herself. 'Oh, I'm just so used to them. It's an old variety that hardly anyone's heard of these days. Petersbirne. There are lots of old trees up in the orchard. The ... previous owner,' she hesitated slightly, 'liked that kind of thing. Old fruit varieties. All kinds of ancient fruits. Their other name is honey pear.'

'They have names?' Sally was surprised.

'"Souvenir du Congrès". "Duchess Elsa". "Madame Verté".' Liss found herself grinning as she listed the names. '"President Douard". "Schweizer Wasserbirne"...'

'Water pear? Honestly?'

'Honestly.' Now Liss laughed out loud.

It was the first time Sally had seen her this liberated.

'Will you show me some time?'

Liss nodded with a smile.

'I thought we'd take the tractor.' Sally was a little surprised when Liss wheeled a very dusty mountain bike out of the barn and put it in front of her.

'No need,' Liss answered briefly. She took a sack from the hook by the gate and wiped down the crossbar, saddle and handlebars with it.

'Needs pumping up,' she said, walking back into the house. Sally looked at the tyres. The bike hadn't been used for a long time. It was too small for Liss, she realised as she cautiously swung a leg over the bar, but it was perfect for her.

Liss came back and knelt next to the bicycle. Sally liked the way she moved. It was exact, in a casual way. Precise, but not like a machine ... accurate. Accurate, that was the word.

A few minutes later, Liss said, 'Done,' stood up and folded up the pump. 'Have a test ride.'

Sally set off on a lap of the farmyard.

'OK,' she said, 'that's OK.'

Liss nodded and fetched her own bike.

This time they headed out of the village by the main road, going southward, past the sole bakery, past the old farms. Standing in one of the front gardens was an old woman, hoeing her flowerbeds. When she saw Liss, she looked up, smiled and nodded to them both. Then she went on hoeing, and it was only then that Sally realised no one else in the village ever greeted Liss.

To the north was an estate that was all new houses and right-angled streets, but here the village looked much as it probably had sixty years ago – if you ignored the cars standing in the cobbled yards, outside the massive, slate-roofed barns. And it wasn't like the city. When you got to the edge, the village really stopped. A track turned off to the right, towards the woods. Sometimes there was maize on either side, as tall as a man, and then it was like cycling down an alleyway. At other times they rode past empty fields. They looked sad in the grey air, and although it wasn't at all cold, Sally found herself thinking about autumn.

'Where did you get this bike?' she asked Liss, who was riding in silence, two bike-lengths ahead.

Liss didn't answer at first and didn't drop back to have a conversation.

'All kinds of stuff collects on a farm like mine,' she eventually called back over her shoulder.

For the first time, Sally had the feeling that Liss was being evasive.

'Was it your husband's or what?'

Liss didn't answer.

'Your husband's? Or your boyfriend's? Did you used to be married?'

Liss didn't answer again. A cold little desire rose up in Sally. She pedalled harder and caught up. She was riding beside Liss now.

'What's up with him? Where is he? Tell me!'

Liss braked. Sally reacted quickly, but even so, she was several metres ahead of her by the time she came to a stop. She turned her bike to look at Liss. Her tanned skin looked copper in the hazy light. She was breathing rapidly and opened her mouth to say something, but shut it again, then, in a voice that buzzed with great tension, she said:

'We won't talk about that bicycle.'

Sally stared at her. She recognised this moment. Sometimes you pushed people too far. Sometimes you broke through their defences.

'Why not? What's wrong with the bike? What's wrong with your husband? Why won't we talk about it?'

Liss looked down for a moment. Sally noticed that she was gripping the handlebars so tightly her knuckles were glowing white.

'I expressed myself badly.' Liss was still speaking in that almost metallic voice. 'I won't talk about that bicycle. If you want, you can go back.'

She raised her head and looked at Sally. Sally couldn't read anything in her eyes. She held her gaze. She could do that. She was good at it. The others always looked away first. But Liss didn't even engage in the fight. She hurled herself abruptly onto the saddle and started to pedal, riding past Sally towards the forest, without looking back.

'Are you afraid of me?' Sally shouted after her. 'Are you afraid? What's the fucking deal with the bike? Did he leave it behind when he left?'

Liss jumped off the bike so fast that she stumbled, and her cycle clattered onto the track. In a few strides she was with Sally.

'Don't!' she hissed. 'Don't do that. Ride or don't ride, but don't talk about this bicycle.'

Then she turned around, picked up her bike and rode on.

But Sally got off and let the mountain bike fall. Suddenly she had wet eyes and she hated herself for it. Crying softened everything up. Crying made you weak. She kicked at the bike but caught her ankle on the pedal. Hot and sharp, the pain shot up her leg. Yes. Still better than crying, she thought, biting her teeth together, still better than crying.

She pulled the bike up and got on again. She didn't want Liss thinking she'd go back now. She wasn't that weak. The ankle stung with every stroke, and that was good. She pedalled faster and harder, stood up and rode out of the saddle. The wind dried her eyes. When she reached the edge of the woods, her lungs were burning so fiercely that she could no longer feel the ankle, and she was just in time to see Liss disappearing between the trees.

'What does tagging mean?' Sally asked gruffly once she'd caught up with Liss. The latter was standing by a tree, spraying two neon lines on the bark. Liss looked at her for a second, then half turned towards the tree that she'd just marked.

'You mark the trees to be felled. And the others that you want left standing.'

'Why them too? If you don't mark them, they'll be left standing anyway.'

Liss pushed her bike on a bit and looked into the treetops. Sally followed her gaze. The clouds had started to break up a little. You could see patches of blue here and there now. The crowns of the trees were still dense; only a very few leaves had turned yellow. Liss sprayed another mark on a trunk.

'Sometimes you want a sapling to have enough light to grow,' she explained briefly. 'Then you have to make space. If you want certain deciduous trees in the forest, for example. Spruces and pines grow faster than oaks or beech trees.'

Sally had a thought. She smiled maliciously.

'You mean, you fell the tall, old trees so that the young ones can grow? I like that.'

Liss gave a dry smile. You could barely see it.

'If they're sick or too old, yes. And you mark the young ones to make sure they don't get accidentally felled by the skidder when the logs are cleared out of the woods.'

They wheeled the bicycles on over the soft forest floor. Now and then the tyres jolted over roots. It smelt different here. And it was a lot quieter.

'Where are the birds? I can't hear anything at all.'

Liss looked at her in surprise.

'You notice that?'

Sally was surprised too, but she didn't want Liss to see it. Was she so ... was it so obvious that she was a city girl?

'Have they gone already?'

'Some have,' said Liss. 'But most have just stopped singing. The vast majority of birds only sing during the mating season and while they're brooding. For me, spring is over when I can't hear the larks. They only sing until July.'

Sally thought about when she'd last been in a wood. Must have been a while ago. The only times she could remember were class trips from primary school. They'd made such a big deal about being alternative; they'd shown them beetles and maggots and stuff that lived under the bark. And they'd made fires and cooked campfire bread on sticks. Had she always hated it, even then? Perhaps she'd never been able to enjoy anything other people liked.

Liss walked beside her in silence. Now you could hear the occasional bird, but not singing. Just a kind of short cry. Under their tyres, dry twigs cracked. Sometimes Liss stopped and sprayed her lines. Then Sally waited. The silence around them grew deeper but not heavier. It was good that neither of them needed to say anything. The forest was changing now. It was lighter, but the trees were taller and looked a lot older. They were all broadleaved trees. Sally stumbled over a stone that jutted out of the soft ground.

'You ought to cover your head,' said Liss, 'you're in church.'

Sally looked at her, mystified. Liss pointed to the stone.

'We're in a ruin. There used to be a village here. A couple of hundred years ago. And you're standing in the church.'

Sally knelt down in fascination. There'd been a village here. There was no sign of it now. Somehow, she'd always thought that towns and villages would be there forever. Sure, they must get built at some time, but she'd never heard of abandoned villages in her own country before. There were no volcanoes here, no sea or anything like that.

'OK. I like standing in this kind of church,' she said, putting her foot on the stone. Maybe it had been the bell tower – submerged in leaves and soil.

'I thought as much,' said Liss.

When they emerged from the forest, onto the edge of a maize field, almost two hours later, Sally had no idea where they were. Liss mounted her bike. The direction felt wrong to Sally, but once they reached a slight peak, she could see the village and get her bearings again. They'd harvested potatoes here. Apparently, they'd gone almost in a semicircle through the woods. As they passed the field, Sally saw the sack. Liss had gathered up all the potatoes except the ones Sally had spilt. The sack was still lying in the furrow, in a little sea of potatoes. It looked unfinished. Sally looked at Liss, who was cycling ahead of her without even a glance at the field. Sally slowed down and, for a moment, she felt the rage again, like an echo. Had Liss brought her along here on purpose? Was this her revenge? But then she saw Liss just riding on, not turning around. Sally, on the other hand, was dropping further and further back, until she braked, got off and let the bike drop into the grass at the edge of the field. For a while she stood there. She didn't know exactly what she was feeling. Maybe just that something wasn't right. By contrast, seeing was easy. It was easy to see what wasn't right here. She crouched in the furrow and began to put the potatoes in the sack, one by one, till there were none left. She found the cord that Liss had thrown down. It was damp and hard to knot. Then she tried to lift the sack of potatoes. She could raise it a little off the ground, but it was far too heavy to carry. She thought. Then she got her bike, laid it in the furrow so that the wheels were against the bank. She hauled the sack halfway over the crossbar, then grabbed the saddle and handlebars and pulled the sack up, using the bicycle as a lever. Breathlessly, she held the bike in balance for a moment, then she began to wheel it out of the field, back onto the track.

Liss rolled the barrels into the middle and lifted them onto the low racks. Here in the cellar, it was so chilly that she shivered a little, even though the sun had now finally come out and was casting a bright beam of light through the chute, so that it slanted across the room. The bottles on the shelves shimmered green. For a moment, as she lifted the lids, the soft scent of the wooden barrels rose gently through the damp air, but it faded as she moved. Liss straightened up and breathed deeply. There were days when it was harder only to see what was actually there. Not to look back, not to look ahead. Just see what was there, right then. Because nothing that existed, at any given point, had just sprung out of nothing, and it wouldn't just vanish into nothing either. Everything had a history. Even inanimate objects acquired a story.

What kind of history did the girl have? She didn't actually want to think about that, but she couldn't help it. The girl was there, bringing a story with her. There were the scars on her legs. Some people had external scars, others had internal ones. Did she have brothers and sisters? She shook her head at herself. Don't ask. It was always better not to know the history. Every question and every answer spun a thread between her and the girl. If you knew everything about a person, you could hold them by a thousand threads.

As her father had her.

She lit the first sulphur wick and threw it into the barrel. The barrels weren't the same as they'd been a year ago. They'd enriched themselves with life. Yeasts. Bacteria. Mould. But it was a type of life that was bad for the wine. You had to burn it out or the wine would go bad.

There'd been threads, wicks, cords, ties everywhere. Visible and invisible. Around a young tree to make it grow straight. She'd asked once why trees had to be straight, seeing that they bore fruit either way, and she'd had to spend two afternoons scratching weeds out of the grouting on the edge of the road. Because it's what you do. Because that's how it is. Because it's not acceptable for everything just to grow however it likes. Even now, after all those years, the hatred blazed up from out of nowhere, from her belly up into her throat, making her gag. She had cut the ties far too late. A tree could no longer grow as it wanted to when it was already tall.

It was starting to stink intensely of sulphur. She lit the second wick. It was an alluring idea, being able to burn the wrong kind of life out of yourself, like you could from a barrel.

A shadow in the beam of sunshine changed the light in the cellar for a moment. Up there, someone was walking across the yard. Liss climbed on one of the shelves, held onto one of the posts, and stood up for a moment so she could see through the chute. It was Sally – she could see her legs and the fine scars on her thighs. She pushed the bike into the barn.

The bike.

The bike was new when Peter plunged down through the vineyard on it. The first warm day in a spring that smelt of awakenings and new beginnings. The sun on his fair hair as he stood up on the pedals, up on the ridge, holding the bike in balance but not setting off. A moment full of desire, when you drew out your happiness a little longer. The vineyard still had the bareness of March, but you could feel the coming spring everywhere, and the wind blew up from the river, ruffled Peter's hair as he stood on the pedals and felt Liss's eyes on him, let go of the brakes and started to roll. He couldn't go fast enough. He could never go fast enough. He pedalled hard, began to plunge down the narrow path as if he wanted to fly across the river at the bottom. Liss followed him on her bike, laughed when vine tendrils whipped her, let herself drop down the steep track after Peter, who took his hands off the handlebars and spread his arms as if he really wanted to fly, and when Liss saw that, her gut lurched. Fly, she urged him in her thoughts, don't fall! Just fly. And he didn't fall, but braked at the foot of the hill, skidding in a little fountain of sand. And dropped along with the bike into the dry grass, which was still yellow from winter, and she had to laugh, because days like that, full of wind and sun and freedom, were so rare.

Liss wobbled for a moment on the shelf. It wasn't so good to think like that. She climbed down. She fetched the mash tubs and stacked them one inside another. She fetched the harvesting baskets and laid them in the tubs. She fetched the pruning shears. Then she grasped the tubs and hoiked them up to carry them to the yard. They were heavy, but that suited her just then.

As she pushed the outer cellar door open with her hip, she saw Sally, who was about to walk into the house. Sally saw her too and came over without hesitation to help her with the tubs.

'Where to?' she asked, gripping the other side.

'Just in the middle, by the drain,' said Liss. 'We have to wash them out and leave them in the sun to dry.'

'What are they for?' Sally asked.

'For the mash. In a week or two we'll need them for the pears, if this weather holds.'

She saw that Sally didn't immediately understand what she meant.

'Mash,' said Liss. 'You distil it into schnapps.'

Sally pulled the tubs apart from each other and placed them in a semicircle around the drain. Liss walked over to the barn, to fetch the hose. When she swung open the door, she saw the sack of potatoes standing by the bike, and it took her a moment to understand. Then, unthinking, she went over and ran one hand tenderly over the smooth, cool steel, and the other over the rough warmth of the jute sack. Feeling the two sensations at once filled her with pain, a strangely beautiful pain.

8 September

Sally was coming out of the henhouse, carrying the eggs in the crook of her arm, when the Golf drove onto the farm. She didn't know whether the driver had seen her, and she shouldn't have actually cared. Even if he had. He'd seen her. What could happen? All right. Tell yourself you don't care. I don't care.

No.

She did care. She didn't want to be seen. She didn't want to keep running. Not today. She walked hastily over to the old wooden silo. There was a ladder up the outside, and there were hatches at regular intervals, all standing open. There weren't any cows anymore, so Liss probably didn't need the silo. She was still constantly amazed at the number of buildings on a farm like this. Stables. Barns. Sheds. She set the eggs down and then climbed a little way up the ladder. When she got to the second hatch, she sat on the edge and hooked her feet in the rungs. From here, she could just see into the yard, past the gable end of the stable, yet she herself was almost invisible. When she leant back a little, she found herself smiling in surprise. In the empty tower, all the village noises suddenly sounded as though they were coming from an old radio.

The driver had not got out. He just hooted briefly, twice. Sally waited, but nothing happened. After a minute, there was another hoot. Somewhat longer this time, and now Liss appeared. Her face was harder than Sally had ever seen it. She kind of liked that. But it was spooky all the same. She watched as Liss bent down to the car window. She couldn't hear what the driver said, but she heard Liss's gruff 'no' very clearly. It echoed around the tower. Sally gripped the rusty ladder-upright with one hand and leant forward a little. Liss had walked into the house and slammed the door behind her. The driver got out of the car. He carried himself like an old man. An old fart, thought Sally. It seemed apt. His trousers were too loose, and the blue jacket he wore was too big. He followed Liss into the house. The village was very quiet. Above her, a couple of swifts whirred through the air. In the city, she'd always thought they were swallows. Liss had been the first person to tell her they were swifts. You didn't generally get very many in the country because they needed towers or tall houses, but the farm was next to the church. Nine months. She still didn't believe what Liss had said, that swifts could stay in the air for nine months without ever landing. Sleeping. Eating. Drinking. Everything happened in the air. That's how you ought to be. Never having to go back to the ground.

The kitchen door opened, and the man came out again. He had a cardboard box in his arms. Liss followed close behind him. For the first time, Sally heard her raise her voice.

'Not that!' she said in a loud, metallic voice. 'You're not taking that.'

'It hasn't belonged to you for a long time,' the man retorted furiously. 'It's all his.'

He put the box on the back seat and wanted to get in. Liss was in his way. Sally watched in fascination as the old man tried to push her aside. Liss simply stood there. In the end, he moved surprisingly rapidly, ducked under and past her, and jumped into the car.

'Get back here!' Liss screamed with rage, but the car was already reversing. Sally watched as, almost without looking, she reached for the spade leaning against the house wall and drew the sharp edge along the whole length of the car as it drove past her. Slivers of paint sprayed out, shining in the sun. The brake lights lit up. The door half opened, but Liss whacked the spade onto the lid of the boot, and yelled:

'What are you going to do now? Call the police?'

The door shut again and the motor roared. Liss hurled the spade right across the yard.

Wow. What had all that been about? Sally leant back cautiously, far into the hatch. Better if Liss didn't see her right now. That had taken guts. She'd just scratched up his whole car.

'Come down.'

Fuck. She had seen her after all. But her voice was back to normal. Sally climbed down the ladder and walked slowly over to Liss.

'Who was that?'

'An arsehole,' Liss answered perfectly calmly.

'And what was in the box?'

'Books,' Liss said curtly. Her face showed that she didn't want to be asked anything more. Sally just waited.

'They...' Liss hesitated for a moment. 'They're important to me, but they don't actually belong to me. I just thought ... I hadn't thought they'd be fetched now,' she added hastily. 'Would you like some tea?'

'Actually, I want to know who the man was,' answered Sally.

'I told you.' Quite unexpectedly, Liss smiled. 'An arsehole. Come and have some tea.'

Sally followed her into the kitchen. How did this fit together? Liss wasn't like that. But OK, sometime she'd tell her. And, to be honest, she didn't like always being asked things either. It was OK. She got that. Some people were just arseholes who should never have been given a name in the first place. It was OK.

When the tea was ready, they took it out into the yard with

them. Sally sat on the wall that ran around the empty midden and looked up at the swifts in the sky and then back at Liss, who was standing there quite calmly, drinking her tea. Maybe she wanted to be a swift too sometimes.

9 September

Liss studied herself in the wardrobe mirror. It was a long time since she'd worn this dress. More than fifteen years. How clothes changed you. Just fabric and colour – and there stood a stranger. But it was also good to be able to wear what she wanted. She just felt unfamiliar to herself. She stood perfectly still and looked herself in the face, as if she were meeting an old schoolfriend, someone she hadn't seen since those days. What still remained of the withdrawn girl from back then, whose mouth could be set so firm sometimes, if she really wanted something?

In the glass, a shadow slipped past the half-open door. Sally had got up; on the way to the bathroom, she paused and looked into the room at her.

'All in black?'

Liss nodded and looked at her in the mirror. 'I have to go to a funeral.'

She could see that Sally was thinking about what she ought to say. No automatic murmur of 'I'm sorry,' without even knowing who'd died.

'Someone you knew well?'

Sally was also talking to the woman in the mirror. It was as if it were easier to speak this way.

'Old Heuberger. As a child, I always played on his farm when...'

She finished the sentence in her head. When I couldn't bear it here any longer. When I wanted to travel at least one street over, into slight freedom. When I couldn't stand the old smell in this house any longer.

'He hadn't lived in the village for a long time,' she said instead. 'He died in a home. But he insisted on being buried here.'

'Can I come?'

Surprised, Liss looked away from the mirror, straight at the girl.

'You won't...' she began hesitantly, before stating firmly: 'You probably can't go in those clothes. It's not like the city here.'

'You can lend me something,' said the girl, still standing in the door.

Liss opened the wardrobe door. The whole room coasted across the mirror, and she beckoned Sally in.

♠

She liked the bells. The very first night she'd slept here, she'd realised that. Although the church was so close, they never sounded too loud. She'd never paid any attention to church bells in the city, but here she noticed: their tone sounded softer than the ones at home. They rang for much longer here too.

Churches. She couldn't care less about churches. And now she was going to the funeral of a man she'd never even known. Liss had lent her a black skirt. It wasn't entirely suitable because it had a pattern of colourful stripes round the bottom hem – kind of a bit Indian-looking – but at least it was mostly black. But the white blouse she was wearing felt much more peculiar. More like a shirt really. It would never have fitted Liss, it would've been far too small for her. Another of those things...

It was only a few steps from the farm to the church, but there were more people walking that short distance than she'd seen in a week in the village.

'Why are they staring like that?'

A malicious little smile was playing around Liss's lips.

'Because they don't know you.'

Sally saw that some of them were blatantly looking her over, while others quickly turned their heads away if she stared challengingly back.

'And maybe because they're afraid of me. I don't often go to church.'

Sally had figured that much out. Liss didn't seem like a churchgoer. Afraid? Yes, some of them were looking timidly at Liss.

'So why now?'

They'd reached the iron gate in the church wall and, suddenly, they were surrounded by women in black. Many of them were wearing headscarves. Images popped into Sally's head – her father's black-and-white photos of Italy that used to hang in the hall. They showed women like this – in black, with headscarves. And now here she was in the middle of them.

'I liked old Heuberger.' Liss's voice was dry. 'So standing at his grave is what you do.'

It's what you do. What's what you do?

'Nothing is what you do!' Sally said, unexpectedly sharply. 'Just because people have always done a thing doesn't mean you have to...'

She left the sentence unfinished. Liss stopped in the church door. The bells were ringing, and from inside you could hear the organ.

The autumn sun makes her face beautiful, thought Sally, disjointedly.

'Yes,' said Liss, 'you're right. But some things are embedded so deeply within you that you do them anyway. I liked him. He might not've known that, but that's why I'm here. You don't have to come.'

Sally said nothing, but she walked past Liss into the church. It wasn't big. Just a village church. There were only a few seats free, in the rearmost pews. Liss nodded over to her left, and Sally slipped into the pew. Liss stayed standing a moment, then sat down. Everyone who came in after them did the same thing.

'What are they doing?' Sally asked quietly.

'Saying the Lord's prayer before they sit down.'

'This can't be real, can it?' she asked, fairly loudly. Liss looked enquiringly at her. Sally pointed at the pews to the right of the aisle. There were only men sitting there. Here, on the left, were only women and children. Sally almost laughed.

Liss leant over and said quietly: 'That's how it is here. Still.'

Sally was surprised that she wasn't angry. It was a very different feeling. Again, it was like the feeling she'd got from looking at her father's photos. Like you'd plunged into an ancient world, one that lay very close to the real world, but that she'd never noticed. A feeling like ... fascination. Yes. As if you'd walked round a corner you'd known forever and suddenly found yourself in a different country.

She didn't take in any of the sermon. She felt like a researcher. She stood up when Liss stood up and sat down when Liss sat down. She observed the women in their rows of pews and the colourful light falling through the windows onto the black fabric of their dresses. She took a look at the men's faces. Was she just imagining it, or did they really have different expressions here from the men in the city?

Liss didn't sing, but the book lay open in front of her. Sally read the words of the hymns. Had it always been like this for Liss, since she was little? Always going to this church, always in the pews to the left of the door, always the same hymns? If you grew up here, you didn't just have your own history, you had the whole village history behind you. Maybe sometimes it even felt good to be a part of the whole. To be the village and not herself. She was scared by the idea.

Standing at the front was the open coffin, on two trestles wrapped in black cloth, inclined slightly towards the congregation. Sally had never seen a dead person before. His face was yellow and looked a bit like a bird of prey. Sharp. Not evil, but sharp. She was surprised when four men stepped forward, lifted the lid onto the coffin, screwed it down with rapid movements and then picked the whole thing up.

'What happens now?' she asked Liss quietly.

'We walk to the cemetery,' she answered, standing up. She left the hymn book behind.

The men carried the coffin down the aisle, and everyone stood up. As they moved, the hundred dresses and hundred suits sounded like the rushing of a wave, breaking in the quiet of the church.

Whoa, Sally thought to herself, whoa. She had no idea what she liked about it. Perhaps that nobody had to tell them what to do. Everyone knew when to stand up. Everyone knew that they had to wait until the coffin had passed before they stepped out of the pews; the front rows first, and then the others, one pew at a time. It was a bit like ... yes, a bit like a ballet.

They'd sat right at the back so they were pretty much at the end of the procession.

'Nice to see you, Elisabeth,' an elderly voice said, next to Sally. It was an old lady, very small, who had spoken to Liss. Aha, Elisabeth. OK. She'd have called herself Liss too, if her parents had named her that.

Liss merely nodded.

'Quite uncalled for,' muttered another voice. 'Shameless. Shameless!'

Sally saw that Liss tensed, but she didn't turn to the other woman. She might have been a bit older than Liss. Bitchy face. And she'd said it loudly enough for everyone standing nearby to hear. Sally wanted to say something, but then the elderly voice spoke again:

'In church? Shame on you, Weber Katti.'

'Thank you, Anni.' Liss said it loudly and very clearly.

The old woman nodded.

'We're moving on,' she said in that thin, old voice that still had something solid about it. The procession began to move.

They walked along the village street: a long, black train. It was hot, and wearing black was making Sally sweat. There were apple and pear trees in the gardens they passed. The apples shone amid the deep-green leaves like blobs of paint. How good it felt sometimes just to be alive. Nothing else. Just to be alive.

'Who was that?'

Liss looked enquiringly at her. 'Who?'

'The old lady.'

Liss gave a thin smile.

'Anni.'

Anni. Sally gave Liss a challenging look, but she said nothing else. OK. Don't then.

The procession was making only slow progress. Sally had time to study the houses. Many were clearly older than Liss's. Patches of plaster had fallen off some of the walls, and you could see that they were built of the heavy grey-white limestone from the area.

There was barely a straight wall to be seen, because the plaster couldn't entirely balance out the natural unevenness of the stone. Many of the roofs were topped with slate rather than brick tiles. They had to be incredibly heavy, and Sally wondered what it must be like to grow up with a weight like that over your head. On the other hand, you didn't need a slate roof to feel a weight above you. The air at home was sometimes as heavy as stone. Her shoulders twitched involuntarily ... She didn't want shitty images of home today.

All along the street were children with white handkerchiefs in their hands, one every hundred metres or so, all the way up to the cemetery entrance.

'What are they doing?'

Liss followed her gaze.

'There's no bell at the cemetery chapel,' she answered. 'But when they pray the Lord's Prayer in the chapel, it has to ring. So Anni gives the first boy a sign, and each of them waves their hankie to the next one, up to the church, and then the sexton rings the bells.'

'No way. Don't they have mobiles here?'

Liss smiled again. Again it was only a very thin smile. 'That's the way they've always done it here.'

It sounded unkind. But then she smiled properly and pointed ahead.

'Besides: can you imagine old Anni with a mobile, tapping out a text at the blessing?'

Sally couldn't help grinning.

It was like a film. The sun on the gravestones. The huge chestnut trees in the cemetery, the wind rustling in their crowns, like the sea. The pastor on the thin plank that had been laid right over the grave because the grave was right by the wall. The mumbling of the prayers. The children waving their hankies. The bells, striking up along with the Lord's Prayer. The thud of the earth on the coffin in the grave. And Liss who, without a word, turned to leave as the others started to offer the family their condolences. Sally was so fascinated by the images that she didn't immediately follow her. She watched her stepping between the tall trees to the cemetery exit. Somehow you couldn't describe it any other way. A tall, slim woman, all alone on the path. The midday light shimmered around her, and then Sally did have to follow.

They walked in silence, side by side. It was hot, and when a tractor, piled high with bales, chugged past them, there was a smell of dust and of straw.

'Has it always been like that?' Sally asked in the end, as they turned into Liss's farm.

'Always,' said Liss, going upstairs to change. Sally stayed standing in the yard, looking over at the church. The golden ball on the tip of the spire shone in the spotless blue of the sky. What was it even for? And how had Liss sounded just then? Proud? Sad? Mocking? Or just bitter?

She couldn't have said.

11 September

She'd asked Liss if she could borrow the bike. The bike. Why hadn't Liss just said who the bike belonged to? Why hadn't she spoken to her about it? She could've just said ... What could she have just said? My ex-husband? My boyfriend? There was no second toothbrush in the bathroom. Or rather there was, the one she was using now, but that had been in its packet. No razor. No men's deodorant or anything. But there was furniture in the rooms, not much, but still a bed and a desk, and Sally could see that someone else had lived there once. Maybe she'd had a lodger. It was hard to say whether men or women had lived in the other rooms. So she was alone on a farm where more people had once lived. What had happened? And why wouldn't she talk about it? Sally had the feeling that Liss knew a lot more about her than she did about Liss. The longer she thought about it, the funnier that seemed. She wanted to know more about her. For the first time in ages, she wanted to know more about another person. Maybe this needed a different approach. Liss didn't seem to like answering questions.

But then she hadn't felt like staying on the farm, so she'd asked Liss if she could lend her the bike. Liss hadn't answered and, in the end, Sally had simply taken it and ridden cross-country until she reached a small town where there was an internet café. She'd been without her phone for over a week now and, however much she resisted, she was missing it. The phone had been part of her life for so long ... on the farm she'd had the feeling of being completely cut off. Liss did have a laptop, but Sally hadn't felt any desire to ask if she could use it. And besides, she needed to get out. It was never good when she didn't move. Maybe she'd already been on the farm for far too long. But then again, it was good there: she didn't know of any other place like Liss's farm for not trying to hold on to her.

She didn't know of anywhere that hadn't tried in some way to tie her down. Home. School. The clinics. As soon as you walked in, the tethers and chains and strings and nets grew out of the walls and out of the floor and down from the ceiling, and it became increasingly difficult to walk around them, and it became increasingly impossible to move away from home and school and her friends' houses, and from everywhere in general. They were supple chains and elastic tethers and rubber nets, but the further you wanted to get away, the more they pulled at you, pulled you gently back; at night they grew sticky and heavy, and you had to keep your mouth shut and breathe through your nose to stop them crawling inside you. Or they stuck to food and you accidentally swallowed them down like a hair, a hair that never stopped growing ever thicker and more rigid and then pulled at you from inside till you had to puke. That was why it was sometimes better not to eat.

But as she'd ridden the bike through the fields and villages, through the clear autumn air, she hadn't felt anything pulling. Liss's farm didn't pull on her. She was still free. She'd bought coffee in the town, and checked her groups from the internet café. It felt funny to see that she wasn't much of a big deal. Someone had written somewhere that she'd run away from the clinic. And Eve – screw Eve – had commented on everything in that 'wow, seriously man I'm so sorry for her' tone. Sally had read that and left the group. Then she'd drunk her coffee. Later, when she'd been wheeling her bike through the streets of a strange town in the afternoon sun, she'd bought a scoop of strawberry ice cream from the ice-cream café and sat at a fountain until it was all eaten. She'd got back in the middle of the night and slept in late and read all the next day. She'd been ten the last time she'd done that.

Today, by contrast, she'd woken up early. After all, she hadn't exactly done anything to tire herself out. She could hear Liss in the bathroom, so it had to be really early. She lay there even though she urgently needed a piss. She waited until she'd heard Liss go downstairs before jumping out of bed and walking over to the bathroom. It was still pretty dark, but she didn't put the light on. That way, the colours stayed as quiet as the morning. She went to the washbasin, turned on the tap, saw the drops of blood on the rim and thought maybe she'd hurt herself without noticing, in her sleep perhaps; sometimes she scratched the tops off mosquito bites and didn't notice, but there was nothing on her face. She scooped water with both hands and poured it over the stains; the blood dissolved slowly, washed into the plughole and disappeared. She splashed her face with water, cold water. When cold water touched your forehead, it set off a reflex. The tall doctor had explained that once. Cold water in your nose or on your forehead. Like in babies. The heartrate slowed and the breathing stopped. If babies fell into water, they didn't drown. Or not right away, anyway. As for her ... she always felt her heart slowing when she washed her face with ice-cold water. Her breathing stopping so that, for a moment, she couldn't breathe even if she wanted too. It was a good feeling.

She got dressed and went down to the kitchen. Liss was sitting at the table, one leg drawn up onto the chair, eating fruit and yogurt, and drinking tea.

Sally mumbled good morning and sat down on the bench. She reached out a hand for the teapot, but Liss moved faster and passed it to her. Liss had a bandage around her left forearm, the blood hadn't soaked through but she could see it shimmering in three places: reddish, longish marks. It was immediately familiar to Sally because she'd seen that so often on herself.

Her first impulse was to stand up and tip the teapot over, or smash it on the floor. What was that about? Was it a kind of ... what *was* that? How sick was that? Did she want to...

'Hey!' she said aloud. 'Hey, what ... what the ... what is that shit? Are you playing at...' She didn't know what it was. She pointed at Liss's arm. 'Do you think that's funny or what? Is that ... what the fuck?' she repeated when words failed her.

Liss had put the newspaper down. She ran her right hand gently over the bandage.

'I wanted to know what it was like,' she said calmly. 'I couldn't imagine ... I wanted to know how it feels.'

'And?' Sally yelled, but it was totally not the fury she was familiar with, it was a different kind of fury. Like ... furious sympathy. She hated it. She wanted to be furious. Just furious. 'And? Does it turn you on, being a psycho, huh? Welcome to the club. Welcome to the cutter club.'

Liss stood up and fetched the honey from the cupboard before answering.

'It hurts.'

'Of course it hurts,' Sally exclaimed. She wanted to yell, but she wasn't angry enough anymore. She was just raising her voice now. 'Of course it hurts. What did you expect?'

'Nothing. That's why I tried it. Would you like some honey?'

'No.'

Sally gulped her tea.

'Yes.'

Liss handed her the jar. Sally unscrewed the lid and dunked her knife, twisting it as she drew it out to stop the honey dripping, and then used the knife to stir it into her tea. Liss looked at her.

Sally stared challengingly back. She laid the knife on the plate. Suddenly she grinned:

'You don't have to go and copy that too.'

Liss laughed as if she'd been liberated. 'Would you like to see where it comes from?'

'What?'

Liss pointed at the honey.

'You make it yourself?' Sally asked in surprise, before continuing hastily, with a crooked smile: 'That was stupid, OK. But have you really got bees?'

Liss stood up. 'In the garden.'

Sally drank up her tea and followed her outside.

How luminous these September days could be! She couldn't remember ever having found an autumn this beautiful. OK, when she was little there'd sometimes been days at the end of the holidays that had had a bit of what she was feeling today. But it was as if it were the other way around, as if what she'd sensed back then had been a faint echo of the emotion she was feeling so intensely today. What was in this September glow, this boundless sky, this morning? It was as though the world wanted to show her once more how beautiful it could be, how many colours it had, how fresh it could smell.

Liss walked ahead of her with the calm, casual, long stride of a tall woman who had no problem with her height. Sometimes Sally thought that walk was pretty cool. It was stupid to kid yourself. Nobody would notice either way. Until Liss suddenly stumbled, making Sally laugh. The hens were so stupid; they always managed to run between your legs, so that it was genuinely difficult not to step on them. Liss turned to her with a smile.

'Most accidents happen in the house or yard ... including to chickens.'

'Yes,' Sally answered mischievously, 'it's a miracle chickens have survived evolution to this point.'

Liss walked round the corner past the machine shed.

'Here.'

In the corner between the fence and the roughly plastered, windowless wall of the machine shed were a row of boxes stood on legs, standing in the semi-shade of a large bush.

'Those are the hive entrances.' Liss pointed to the narrow slit at the bottom of every box. Sally had barely been able to make them out at first because there were so many bees everywhere, coming in to land, taking off, buzzing, closely packed, crowding, crawling over one another and forming a compact cluster outside every hive. Sally crouched down in front of one. It almost looked like a morning on the U-Bahn. Everyone milling out, everyone milling in. She had never seen so many bees so close before. After a while, she could make out some kind of order. At any rate, they managed the take-offs and landings with fewer collisions than the commuters on her rush-hour underground journeys.

'Can we collect some honey?' she asked, still watching the bees.

Liss shook her head.

'Far too late. You harvest honey in July. The bees' year is almost over. But we still have to have a look inside. Oh, I forgot something. Can you get some icing sugar from the pantry? There's a packet on the butcher's block.'

'For the bees?' asked Sally.

'Yes,' Liss smiled, 'but not the way you think.'

Sally ran back to the house. I'm part of something right now, she thought. I don't know exactly what. I'm part of this sunny day now. I'm part of Liss's work now. I'm part of this house now.

She wasn't at all sure whether that was a good thing. But at that moment, it felt right.

Icing sugar. She'd only been in the pantry once. Here you could still see that there must have been a much older house on this site. Below the window, the floor bulged – the cellar steps were probably beneath it. It looked kind of archaic. As she took the packet of icing sugar from the butcher's block, she saw the knives hanging there, with their dark-stained wooden handles. Without thinking, she reached for one and held it in her hand. You could feel from the handle that it had been used ten thousand times before. It felt very good. For a moment, she simply wanted to have it, simply to pocket it, but then she hung it back up. She could always ... she could always ask Liss about it.

When she got back to the beehives, Liss had spread a piece of canvas on the ground. Standing beside it were a white plastic bowl full of water and two see-through measuring cups, one of which had a sieve for a lid. Sally hadn't a clue what all this was for.

'You're not afraid of being stung, I presume.'

Liss glanced over at Sally, who shook her head.

'But we'll put these on anyway,' said Liss as she reached for the two hats in the grass beside her. Sally put one on. The veil fell softly over her face. Liss handed her a pair of gloves too.

'In case you accidentally put your hand into the bees.'

Now she was intrigued.

'We have to work fast now,' explained Liss. 'We're going to sugar the bees, you see.'

What? Was Liss winding her up? Was this some kind of secret language? But then she saw that one corner of Liss's mouth was twitching half mockingly.

'Yes. Seriously. You'll see. Watch out, I need you to hold the measuring cup – not the big one, that one there' – she pointed at the container without the lid – 'right under the tarp so I can shake the bees into it. We need a hundred mills precisely.'

'For real?' Sally looked up suspiciously. 'We need a hundred millilitres of bees?'

'Yes,' said Liss briefly. 'That'll be five hundred of them, give or take a few.'

'Whatever you say,' said Sally, picking up the cup. It measured exactly a hundred millilitres. 'And then what do I do?'

'You tip them into the big jug and put the lid on. Ready?'

Liss didn't even wait for her to answer. All at once she was moving very fluidly, confidently and as if every handhold was exactly where it should be. She opened one of the hives, pulled out a panel that was covered all over with bees, layer upon layer of bees, and banged one edge hard onto the canvas. The bees rained down onto it. Liss put the panel away, picked up the cloth and folded it, enclosing the bees in a kind of bundle.

'Now,' Liss ordered, and Sally held the jug under one corner of the folded tarpaulin, Liss tipped it and poured bees into Sally's container.

'Stop,' said Sally when the cup was full; she was already holding the other one when she felt a sharp pain in her forearm. A bee had stung her. She resisted the temptation to brush it off, tipped the contents of the small jug into the big one, dropped the little one and put the lid on. Liss dropped the rest of the bees from the tarpaulin almost carelessly back into the hive. Sally rubbed her arm. It was ... It hurt, but it was a strangely good feeling. Liss took the cup from her hand.

'Now the sugar. Quick. If the bees are in there too long, it'll get damp.'

Sally handed her the sugar. Liss dusted a little – maybe a spoonful – onto the sieve and shook. The sugar fell down onto the bees in the container, made them dusty; they were all powdered white with icing sugar.

'What … why are you doing that?' She was no longer suspicious, just fascinated.

'Hang on,' answered Liss, looking at the watch on her wrist. It was a man's watch. It suited her. She shook the jug hard, waited quite a while, shook it again while keeping her eyes on her watch, and then again.

'The bowl,' she said.

Sally reached for the white plastic water bowl and was about to hand it to her, but Liss waved her away, upended the measuring cup over the bowl and dusted the water. The sugar instantly dissolved. A few black dots were floating in the water.

'Shall I pour it away?' asked Sally.

'No!' cried Liss, almost alarmed. 'No. Wait a moment.'

She took off the lid, went over to the hive and shook the bees cautiously out again. Then she took the bowl from Sally's hand and put it on the next hive along.

'The black dots,' she explained, 'are mites. Varroa mites. They can destroy a colony of bees within a year. And they're everywhere. I need to know how bad the infestation is to know whether the bees need treating. Count them.'

Sally leant over the bowl.

'Fifteen,' she said. 'No, sixteen. What's the sugar for?'

'The mites cling to the worker bees. The icing sugar makes them lose their grip. And because it dissolves immediately in water, you can make out the mites.'

Sally wondered how anyone had come up with such a bizarre idea as dusting bees with icing sugar so you could see mites. The weirdest thing of all was that it seemed to work.

'What now?'

Liss counted again.

'Yes. Sixteen. That's right on the limit. We'll have to treat them, but not necessarily today. And we'll have to check the others too.'

'OK,' said Sally. She rubbed the sting. It had already stopped hurting. She looked into the hive. That was awesome. That was so awesome! The sugared bees were being cleaned by the others. She began to understand why Liss had bees. Maybe it wasn't just about the honey. Maybe it was about ... discovering something. The way she'd done just now.

'Ready?' asked Liss. She'd spread the tarpaulin in front of the other hive. Sally picked up the cup.

'Ready,' she said.

For the first time in months, she was happy for a moment.

Your parents aren't that shit.

You have no idea.

No. They're nice.

Yes. Exactly.

She and Ben were sitting on the bike racks outside the shopping centre. Everyone went there. They listened to music. They watched YouTube videos of dancing cats and ones where little kids on tricycles were put on low diving boards by their parents and then pedalled to the end of the boards and fell in the water. It was kind of mean, but it still made them laugh every time.

Why do we laugh at it?

Because it's funny.

Ben was right. It was kind of funny. And kind of not.

It's like my parents, she said.

What?

What you said. Them being nice. It's kind of true and kind of not at all.

All parents are like that. Mine too.

No, she said, you don't understand. Your family's different.

Want an ice cream? I'll get you one.

No. Hey, are you even listening?

Ben was already heading to the kiosk to get ice cream. Over the road was the bus station. The waiting buses sometimes seemed to Sally like large, sleeping animals, breathing slowly. But she never said that kind of stuff. Not even to Ben.

The other girls glanced fleetingly over to her. When Ben wasn't there, their expressions were different. They went back to normal. When he was around, they meant: how did *she* bag *him*? She didn't even know herself. Ben actually played tennis. She'd never wanted a boyfriend who played tennis. But maybe she just had to take what she could get, she thought mockingly, and found herself grinning.

How's it going with you guys?

Eve strolled past. I'm-playing-grown-ups pretty. She even had a clutch bag, which had probably contained the same condom for months, nestled beside her pink mobile. Eve wanted Ben, and she probably still didn't understand what he was doing with Sally.

Hey guys, what's up?

Nothing.

I can tell.

Get lost, Eve. Is bugging me your only goal in life? What will you do when I'm dead?

Eve grinned.

Console Ben.

Fuck you, bitch.

Fuck yourself. Oh no, actually don't. Nobody wants to do you. So why should *you* have to bother?

She strolled on. Arse waggling. Sooo casual. Sooo pseudo-sexy. Sally jumped down from the bike rack. She longed to throw something at her, but there weren't even any stones around here. Such a nice, clean city.

Ben came back. He was licking an ice cream and holding the other one out to her.

I brought you one anyway. Want it?

Give it to Eve, she spat.

Why? What's wrong?

Why not check with my parents?

I don't know what this is all about, said Ben.

No, you don't.

She ran between the buses to the footbridge that led over the ridiculous stream and to the cemetery. Ben followed her.

Sal, wait! Wait a minute.

She ran on, down the cycle path. Tall poplars on either side. At the cemetery entrance was a bench she liked. She liked to watch the people going to the cemetery. When you came here, everything was clear. On both sides. One lot were dead. The other lot came to visit. There was no more room for misunderstanding.

Sheesh, gasped Ben, what did you run like that for?

I don't feel at home.

Sally said it abruptly, almost pleadingly. She wanted Ben to understand her. She climbed onto the bench and sat on the back.

Do you know what that's like? I'm not at home when I'm at home.

I get that.

He didn't get it; Sally could see that. But she wanted him to understand her. There was nobody else.

I'm like ... like a guest. My parents are nice to me like I'm a guest. I don't know what to do with what they do. None of it. It's not just ... it's not just because they listen to different music and do other stuff and that. They don't understand what goes on inside me. They don't understand...

She hesitated.

Sometimes I listen to a song and it's like if a back door opens a tiny crack, somewhere right on the other side of the house, and I hear it from my room and start running because I know that it's there behind the door, my real home. But before I've even got down the stairs, it's shut again.

But you've only got the front door.

Aren't you listening?

Sally was almost screaming with despair.

It's just ... doesn't that ever happen to you? Sometimes music does that and sometimes a picture and sometimes it's just some place, like here among the tall trees. Then you know that your real life is there somewhere, and not this one here. Then you suddenly know that all this here is like a ... a film or a play or something. That none of it's real. Don't you ever get that?

Sometimes.

You never get that.

Sally felt empty.

Yes I do. But not the way you do, I don't think.

No. I don't think so either. Can you ... Do you want to sit here? With me? I like it when people go to the cemetery. They all have a particular face. Shall we watch people?

Why don't we go back to the others?

Sally looked into the young leaves on the poplars. Above them the sky was still bright. The long spring evenings were the worst. Then it tugged at her, from deep within, and she thought that one day, if she didn't follow the tug, it would pull her insides out. Maybe that was what homesickness was like. She'd never been homesick when she'd been on a school trip or a residential or a summer camp. It was probably homesickness for the place you actually ought to be. For a home that you didn't even know yet, but which was waiting for you. Sally was afraid that it wouldn't wait forever and that she'd end up broken because it tugged at her too hard, that she'd end up inside out, with all her delicate innards on the outside, and then it would be too late because you couldn't live inside out.

OK. Let's go back to the others.

13 September

Liss had gone to the village shop by bike. She'd collected a parcel from the post office – a new refractometer – and as she rode over the wet cobblestones, it and the milk bottles rattled in the basket on the pannier rack. She took the shortcut over the pavement and hopped the bike over the kerb, making the bag of croissants jump up with a rustle. It was a cheerful sound, and Liss noticed with surprise that she was looking forward to breakfast with Sally. How quickly you got used to not being alone again. How nice it could sometimes be to shop for someone other than yourself, and to make breakfast. But immediately she reprimanded herself: think properly. Clearly. Straight.

The girl couldn't stay forever. Her parents were sure to find her eventually. And that was probably right. She pedalled harder. No. That wasn't right. The girl was exactly where she wanted to be. And where she should be. For today, there was no other place. Only here. And today. Something had begun that had not previously been there. And not all parents ... some parents wouldn't search for their children.

She thought about the bees. Sometimes it felt good to work together. Because the other person ensured that you recognised your own place in the whole. All of a sudden, you had a significance in a whole, and weren't simply existing. Yes. She was looking forward to her breakfast with Sally.

When she turned into the farm, her good mood evaporated instantly. A police car was standing beside her tractor, and a policeman was walking around her house, looking for something. Liss jumped off her bike.

'Can I help you?' she asked curtly, almost rudely. She was annoyed at her sudden nervousness. It wasn't as though she'd committed a crime.

The policeman turned to her.

'Good morning,' he greeted her politely, 'I just wanted ... We're looking for a girl. Your neighbour,' he gestured over his shoulder with his thumb, 'he reckoned there's been a girl staying here for a few days.'

Liss twisted her mouth into a cheerless smile.

'My neighbour. Oh, the joys of village life. Idyllic. Everyone looking out for everyone.'

The policeman nodded. 'It's different in the city,' he agreed earnestly.

'Who are you looking for, then?' Liss asked, to gain time. She wanted to think, but her thoughts were as gluey as cold honey.

'The missing person is seventeen, very thin, brown hair. I've got a photo of her, wait a moment.' He pulled out his phone.

Liss leant her bike against the wall of the house and hoped that Sally wouldn't come out into the yard right now. How stiltedly the policeman talked. You wouldn't have believed he was for real.

'Here,' he said, holding out the mobile. Liss recognised Sally at once even though her hair was different and the photo was at least a year old, if not older. She shook her head.

'No,' she said as firmly as she could, 'don't know her. Never seen her. Is she ... Has she done something wrong?'

The policeman put his phone away and made a dismissive sound.

'Oh, no. Run away from a clinic. No idea – depression, drugs, anorexia ... something like that. Suicide risk. That's why we're doing the rounds. So who's the girl with you?'

Liss hoped desperately that he hadn't heard her hasty gulp.

'Oh, right,' she hoped she sounded relaxed, 'her. My niece. She's here for the rest of the holidays.'

'Ah well, we're nearly there,' said the policeman, walking to his car.

Liss looked blankly at him.

'They go back tomorrow, don't they? Tomorrow's the first day for my eldest.'

Liss saw that he was waiting for an answer.

'Congratulations,' she said dryly.

The policeman got in with a smile, started the engine and drove out of the yard. Liss leant on the wall for a moment, weak with relief. And then she felt it clawing at her from deep within, the wild animal inside her, on the rampage after being caged for so long, followed by the fury, which surged up like a suddenly blazing fire. She beat her fist against the rough plaster. She walked into the house. It took her every scrap of self-control not to run.

'Sally!' she shouted the moment she reached the hall. 'Sally.'

It might have been her unusual tone, or the fact that she hadn't raised her voice once since the girl had been in the house; either way, Sally appeared at the top of the stairs at once, looking startled.

'Has something happened?'

Liss took the stairs two at a time and stood right in front of her, closer than she'd ever come before. She was fighting to keep her voice quiet, but not succeeding.

'Did you write the letter?'

Sally looked uncomprehendingly at her.

'I asked if you wrote the letter.' She was shouting again.

Sally drew back a fraction. 'I forgot,' she answered in a tone between defiance and astonishment, which made Liss even angrier.

'How?' she hissed, in a red rage. 'How can you forget a thing like that? How?'

Sally took another step back and looked coldly at Liss.

'I just did. I just forgot.'

Liss trembled. She was fighting back the urge to grab Sally and shake her, and she couldn't breathe deeply either. Her vision blurred.

'I've had a sodding policeman on my farm. Just now. They're looking for you, and all you can say is: *I forgot*.'

She imitated Sally's tone in biting, deeply caustic scorn and waited for Sally to yell back; Liss was quivering with combativity and rage, was ready to hit out before she was hurt, was ready to smash everything between them.

Sally looked at her. Gave her a long stare then simply sat down on the floor in front of her.

'Did you kidnap me? Are you holding me prisoner in your cellar? Did you murder me? You fed me. You gave me a room. The only thing you didn't do was ask where I'd come from. Do you think they'll put you in prison for that?'

Sally was speaking firmly and loudly, but not aggressively. Her words seemed to lag as they pierced the red mist in which Liss was standing. All the same, her voice and the fact that Sally was sitting on the floor, looking up at her while she spoke, began to dissolve the fog. Like the sun on a cold autumn morning, very slowly, little by little.

Liss took a deep breath. She was searching for words. That was how it had always been. She'd always lacked the words. They'd only ever come much later. But this time, her own speechlessness allowed her to comprehend Sally's words. Yes. She had committed no crime. She hadn't done anything wrong, it was all in her head. Nobody could force her to ask Sally her age. She could equally well have been eighteen. But it wasn't just that. The fury was still burning bright within her.

'I don't make any demands of you.' She squeezed the words out furiously. 'Nothing. I know what it's like when you ... when people always want things from you. But we had ... you said you'd write the letter.'

Sally was still sitting down. Liss could see that she was trembling, although her voice sounded controlled.

'I forgot,' she repeated, slowly and clearly. 'Forgot. I didn't mean to. Do you understand? Do *you* understand?'

Liss had words on her chest and in her throat – too many; they all wanted to push past one another, each of them wanted to take the lead, and so they were all getting in each other's way. Sally looked up at her. Their eyes caught.

'I'll write the letter,' said Sally.

'Yes,' Liss finally answered. The word set her throat free. Now other words could get through. But, things being what they are, they were suddenly no longer in a rush. 'That's fine.'

She turned and went downstairs. Weak at the knees, as if she'd been running. The anger was draining away like water in a fishpond where someone had opened the sluices. By the time she reached the foot of the stairs, she felt empty and dirty.

It was a long time since she'd been that irate, she thought despondently, as she walked back out into the farmyard to get the things from her bike basket.

But she'd also been alone for a very long time, her thoughts continued as she took the refractometer down to the cellar.

Maybe it would be better if the girl left soon after all.

Maybe it was better to be alone.

16 September

Liss was standing in the pantry, measuring out rye for her bread. She always baked for two weeks ahead, and somehow it was a good sign that the last batch had only lasted nine days. She tied the brown paper sack up again and pushed it under the butcher's bench. When she straightened up, she felt as though she could smell the stale whiff of blood in the wood, and she shook her head unwillingly. Then she leant down again, until her nose was almost touching the wood. No. It smelt of wood. Nothing else. The smell was only in her head. She looked up at the boning knives hanging over the bench. One was missing. But it had been missing a long time. The steel was hanging from a cord beside the knives. She took it down, reached for one of the knives and sharpened it, the way she'd learnt back then.

Eleven years old? Twelve. She was twelve. She was probably twelve. Yes. The first snow had fallen and thawed right away, and the yard hadn't yet been paved, so it was full of cold puddles. Early December.

Are you coming? he'd shouted across the yard. He had on the white rubber apron that he only wore for butchering. Once, when she'd been little, it hadn't used to bother her. But now it was different. It wasn't that she didn't want to eat meat. She loved the ham. She liked the large bratwursts that they sold by the metre or the half-metre at the autumn wine festivals down in the town. She knew that pigs had to die for that, or cows, but that wasn't it. It was the way he did it. She got dressed slowly, but she was still ready too soon. She walked down the back corridor, took the zinc bucket and the wooden spoon, and stepped out into the open.

The sky was grey and low, and a few solitary wet flakes were falling into the puddles, onto the midden wall and onto his grey-brown cap. They melted immediately.

Her mother pulled the tub over to the high frame he'd welded together out of water pipes. A hose ran out of the half-open kitchen window, across the windowsill into the yard; her mother picked it up and began to fill the tub with hot water. The water steamed like it did in the bathroom when she was supposed to have a bath. The thought repulsed her.

He had a cord in his hand and was shouting something at her; she couldn't hear what, but she knew what she had to do either way, so she shut the gate so that the pig couldn't run away if it slipped out. He vanished into the sty, and the pigs squealed because they thought they'd be fed. But then he came out again, dragging the sow behind him as she kicked against the taut cord with both her forelegs. Yes, she thought, you've never seen the yard before. I'd be afraid too. You've never been outside. Never. Other farmers at least kept their pigs outside half the year. He just laughed at that: churn up your orchards and make more work for you. But on the other hand, his sows sometimes ate their own young, which the other farmers' animals never did. If she'd been born a pig, maybe her mother would've ... Maybe it wasn't even wrong for pigs. If the litter didn't work out for the parents, maybe it was better for it to be eaten. She felt queasy. The wooden spoon smelt of blood. Already. You could wash it as much as you liked, it would always hold the iron tang of blood.

The sow squealed. She wanted to go back into the sty. All she'd ever known. And she was strong. The sow dragged the cord from his hand, and he cursed as she ran off around him, but there was Mother with the rake in her hand, standing by the stable door to fend her off. She turned and galloped through the yard, slipped as she went to sidestep the tub and slid a few metres through the mud on the yard. Elisabeth! he bawled, Elisabeth.

No, she thought. He was running after the sow, which had got up again, and threw himself onto her. Literally threw himself onto her. Two pigs in the muck, she thought, and found herself laughing. The sow squealed.

But by then he'd pulled the bolt gun from his pocket, positioned it and fired. The sow fell. Her forelegs twitched. He stood up, pulled the knife from his belt and looked around for her.

The bucket. Get that bucket here.

She brought it, and he looked up, then he looked at her. You gotta learn this, he said roughly, it's high time. He pressed the smooth handle of the knife into her fingers, closed his fist around her hand and drove it into the sow's neck, accurate and without hesitation. She felt in her hand, in her fingers, the way the knife went through skin and fat and flesh – so easily. The dark blood spluttered into the bucket and she pulled out the knife, dropped it and began to stir so that the blood didn't curdle. The reek of iron was so strong that she longed to spew. On him and on the sow and into the filthy puddles. But she swallowed and stirred. The sow was dead. Five minutes. That was the lucky part. Death came so quickly. She looked up at him and wondered what it would be like if he were lying there. In the dirt. Instead of the sow. Stir, she thought, moving the wooden spoon through the thick blood, stir.

Bake bread. This was now. Bake bread.

She switched the mill on and it was only as she let the rye run into the hopper and the noise started up that she realised it was still very early and she'd wake the girl. But it was too late now. The grain ran grey into the pan, and the scent of the rye percolated, wiping away her memory of the stench of blood. She thought rye smelt nicer than wheat. It wasn't that she didn't like the smell of wheat, but when you milled rye, you could still smell the grass it had once been. A good scent.

The girl's voice behind her made her jump. She hadn't heard the door over the racket of the mill.

'What are you doing?' asked Sally, who must have come straight from bed. She was still in her T-shirt and hadn't even put her shorts on. It took Sally a second to register that that was good; that Sally wasn't thinking about the other day anymore. She had to shout to be heard over the grinder.

'I thought you were drilling. Is that a mill?'

Liss nodded but waited for the rye to run through before answering.

'A grist mill. Over a hundred years old. My grandfather used it before me. It's really intended for animal feed, but I use it for bread. You can't bake cakes with this flour.'

Sally stood beside her and reached into the pan, took a handful of grain and let it run through her fingers.

'Can I try?' she asked.

'Go ahead,' said Liss.

'You always do your own baking, don't you?'

Sally chewed the rye slowly.

'It tastes of ... kind of green,' she said. 'Or a bit like the smell of hay.'

'That's rye,' Liss explained. She fetched the bowl of sourdough starter, which she'd covered with a tea towel.

'How do you do it? Baking bread, I mean.'

Sally sat down on the butcher's bench. Utterly uninhibited, as if the other day had never happened. She braced herself on her hands. She crossed her legs at the ankles. Liss caught a brief glimpse of the white stripes of the scars, but also noticed that her knees no longer stuck out the way they'd done three weeks ago. She saw the thing that had hit her so hard the other day: the raw, powerful, brittle beauty in the girl's thin body.

'I'll show you,' said Liss. She handed her the starter. 'Take the cloth off and have a sniff,' she demanded. Sally took it, pulled off the cloth and lifted the bowl to her nose.

'Vinegar,' she said, 'or ... gone-off apple juice?'

'Then it's OK.'

Liss sniffed too. Wasn't it strange that everything she liked doing involved the transformation of sweetness into something else? Baking bread. Pressing wine. Distilling schnapps.

'It's acetic acids and a little alcohol. You have to make rye go sour or you can't bake with it.'

She scooped out a couple of teaspoons of the leaven and put them in an earthenware bowl, which she covered over. Then she handed the spoon to Sally.

'Try?'

Sally took it and popped it in her mouth.

'It doesn't taste of bread,' she said. 'It's good, but not like bread.'

'That comes next,' said Liss. It was strange to be explaining something.

'What about the flour?' Sally asked, pointing at the rye they'd just ground. 'Doesn't that have to be fermented?'

'You add half of it as it is. Along with the salt and spices. Here. Do you want to?'

Sally came closer. She let Liss show her the spices, chewed on anise and fennel seeds, put too much coriander into the dough before Liss could stop her, and then she began to knead the dough in the bowl. It looked powerful. And again, it was like she wasn't doing it for the first time. Or, thought Liss, she grasped what it was about so quickly. You didn't often have to show her things.

She fetched the casserole dishes. Sally, up to her elbows in dough, looked up in surprise.

'Do you boil the bread?'

Liss looked at the pans in her hand. How strange your habits could seem if someone else questioned them.

'No,' she answered briefly, 'you can bake in casseroles too. I like the shape.'

Sally freed her hands from the dough, watched Liss grease the pans with butter, and tried it again.

'It still doesn't taste of bread.'

'You're impatient,' smiled Liss.

'Not as impatient as you,' Sally answered.

Yes, thought Liss after a moment of surprise, I am. Always have been. But it was strange that the girl could see that so clearly. She threw a handful of sunflower seeds into one pan and a handful of sesame seeds into the other.

'Give them a swirl.'

Sally immediately understood what she meant and circled the dishes so that the seeds were evenly distributed as they stuck to the buttered sides. Then, without asking, she put them down and popped in the dough.

'You can eat the rye as it is,' she mused aloud. 'And the dough. The flour. But people want bread. The rye has to be ground and fermented and shaped and burnt. Then we like it.'

She looked at Liss.

'Sometimes I'd like to be like an animal. Take everything as it comes. Eat what's there, just the way it is. Raw. Move like an animal and live like an animal. Without thinking and…' she hesitated '…without being afraid. Without always being tied to something.'

In silence, Liss cut two crosses in the dough to stop the bread tearing as it rose.

'Yes,' she said slowly, 'sometimes that would be nice. But we're not made for that. We can throw.'

'What?' Sally asked uncomprehendingly, opening the door for her. Liss had a pan in each hand. Sally followed her into the kitchen. Liss pointed to the oven, which she'd already preheated a little, and Sally opened it. Liss put the casseroles in.

'The dough needs to prove for an hour now.' She turned to her. 'Throwing. That's what distinguishes us from all other animals. We can aim a throw. And we can shape things. Ferment flour and grape juice. Make wine. Bake bread. That's no bad thing.'

'But it's unnatural.'

Sally fetched herself a glass of water, sat on the bench and drew up her legs. Liss leant on the terrace doorframe.

'What do you think you are?' she asked, amused. 'You're just as much part of nature as a potato. You're exactly as much part of nature as elephants and beavers and humans. We all change stuff. Elephants turned large areas of Africa into savanna by destroying the forests. Beavers dam rivers and destroy the habitats of mice by flooding meadows. We humans are animals. Clever animals, incredibly skilled at manipulating things. Thinking seems to be an evolutionary advantage, for a certain period. Although in the long term … Either way though, we're animals the same as elephants and beavers. We're not outside of nature just because we can build nuclear power stations.'

'Wow,' said Sally. 'I think that's the most I've ever heard you say. So you mean, you can't just leave things as they are? You change everything around you, just by existing. So then it makes no difference whether you destroy more stuff or less.'

She looked challengingly at her. Liss considered before she spoke. This isn't just a conversation about nature, she thought.

'Everything you do has some kind of effect on others. You need to know that, I think. As for destruction ... Am I destroying anything if I help the bees survive?'

'Yes. You're destroying the mites.' Sally grinned. 'You can't win,' she said. 'Admit it.'

Liss smiled. 'Nobody wins this kind of conversation. People just have them to assure themselves of their convictions.'

The grey of dawn was gradually breaking up. The sky over the barn was growing lighter, and the shredded clouds were gradually turning pink.

'Why do you live alone?' asked Sally.

Liss felt everything close up inside her.

'I don't want to talk about it. I don't ask you questions.'

Sally nibbled on her pear. Unfazed. Calm. Liss wondered how it could be that this girl sometimes exploded with rage at the least provocation, while at other times she could be as tranquil as a stone in the sun.

'That's different. You know all about me anyway.'

Liss was astonished. 'Me? About you?'

Sally raised her shoulders, then let them drop again.

'Not so hard,' she said. 'You read the paper. You talked to the policeman. You can see me. And you say I remind you of yourself when you were young. Not so difficult, is it?'

Liss thought for a moment. Maybe there was something in that.

'I like living alone. And not many people can put up with me. Does it matter?'

Sally put the rest of the pear on a saucer. Liss liked the way Sally ate. There was always something very conscious about it; she never did so casually.

'It wouldn't if you were happy,' she said, standing up. 'But you're not. Can we start baking the bread now?'

Liss felt a heat rising inside her, but she held herself back.

'You're not happy either,' she retorted, composedly. 'Why else would you be here?'

Sally looked at her wide-eyed.

'What?' she asked, utterly taken aback. 'Do you think that? When I arrived, I wasn't happy. Truly not. But right now ... or in the vineyard, in the forest ... otherwise I wouldn't still be here.'

Liss opened the patio door. She didn't know what she was feeling. As she walked through it, she said: 'The bread needs another half-hour yet.'

As she walked across the yard, the girl's remark echoed in her ears.

Otherwise I wouldn't still be here.

17 September

Liss was sometimes afraid of not being able to function. Work was everything. It was good to work because then the daily course of things was like a marked path in the mountains. You knew which way you had to go if you didn't want to fall. Any other route would be dangerous.

She was standing under the walnut tree, looking up into the crown. The tree was as old as her. At this age, a walnut bore the richest fruit. There was so much, she'd been able to harvest half the nuts green, back in June, for the liqueur. And there were still plenty now. The first of them had already begun to fall.

'A good cropping year.'

Liss turned to the fence. Anni had got off her bike. She was as old as the hills, yet she still cycled to the church whenever there was a christening or a wedding or a funeral, to decorate it. To Liss it seemed as though that had always been so. And also as though Anni had always worn the same blue peasant headscarf, the same black apron over the same black work dress. Back then, she'd given her pretzels. Today she still spoke to her. Not everyone did. Anni stood for everything that Liss still loved about her village. It was as though she were from another time. Her bicycle had no gears and was as black as her clothing. How long ago had she been widowed? Liss reckoned back. She'd been nineteen. That was how long Anni had been wearing black.

'A good year,' she answered, picking up a nut.

Had Anni always been so small? She seemed barely able to see over the fence.

'Which is it? Funeral or christening?'

It couldn't be a wedding. Weddings were always on Saturdays.

'Old Gutmann died. Didn't you hear?'

'Who from?' she asked curtly.

Anni nodded. Liss tried to find in her face the woman who'd given her the pretzels almost forty years ago. The woman who'd then been the age she was now.

'Goin' to the woods today?' asked Anni, getting back onto her bike again astonishingly effortlessly.

Liss nodded, not wondering how Anni knew that. Maybe it was just that Anni simply asked, and then you'd always been intending to go to the forest, you just hadn't known it.

'Have you got a pretzel for me?' she asked impetuously.

Anni got off again, as if nothing could surprise her, turned around, the bike between her twisted, elderly legs, fished a stale pretzel out of the basket on the back, and passed it over the fence.

'Take care of the girl,' she said in her brittle old-lady voice, as she mounted and rode on to the church, zigzagging slowly.

Yes, thought Liss, biting into the hard pretzel, I will.

As she was pulling the trailer out of the barn in the early afternoon, Sally arrived from somewhere and stood the bike in the yard.

'Autumn's coming,' said Liss. 'I need to load up some wood. It'd be quicker if you could help.'

Sometimes it was hard to say the right thing in the right tone. Everything could be misunderstood. She got that. She had always misunderstood so much.

Sally climbed onto the tractor without hesitation. But she was silent on the ride up to the forest. Liss turned the tractor off the country lane onto the track between the bare fields. The maize fields lay coarse-stubbled. There were crows on the distant, yellow wheat fields, searching undisturbed for dropped grain. There was a swarm of songbirds in the air. Liss couldn't make out what they were. Although the air was warm, you could feel that autumn was coming. The circular saw clattered around on the trailer as they bounced down the track by the forest, and the noise would have made conversation impossible anyway until they reached the elongated woodpile she'd set up two years before. She got down from the tractor, switched off the engine and opened the tailgate on the trailer. The girl clambered straight down over the drawbar onto the trailer, and Liss felt a strange wistfulness: Sally was moving with such a natural practicality now, as if she'd grown up on the farm. She lent a hand as they lifted down the saw, Liss uncoupled the trailer and turned the tractor.

'Don't we need electricity for the saw?'

The girl's voice sounded a little rusty, as if she hadn't spoken all day. Probably hadn't. Liss hadn't spoken to anyone today either, apart from Anni. She pointed to the power take-off.

'That's the difference between a tractor and a car,' she explained. 'When you're out in the tractor, you've always got a motor, just in case. In the old days, they used traction engines. There's one still standing in the Heubergers' barn.'

'What's a traction engine?' the girl asked while reaching out a hand to connect up the circular saw. She slipped the locking pin through the take-off without needing to ask, and Liss remembered the day she'd first met the girl. It seemed longer ago than it really was.

'A steam engine. Looks a bit like a train, but doesn't run on rails. They used horses to pull it to the field, but then they used it for the same things as this tractor here. To power saws or threshing machines, or even to pull ploughs across the fields.'

The girl straightened up.

'You can show me some time,' she said carelessly, but to Liss it sounded as though she'd said the right thing just then.

Once they'd set the engine to the right number of revs, the afternoon was filled with the mournful tones of the circular saw. Always been a winter sound, thought Liss, as she began to take lumber from the pile, quarter timber by quarter timber, and to cut it. The monotonous singing of the idling blade, the brief screech as it ate its way through the trunk, then the singing again. She couldn't help it: to her, this sound was linked to snow and short days, to cold and winter. Yet it was a warm afternoon, and as the forest shadows lengthened, the cool was welcome. Sally was wearing bright-red ear defenders, throwing the pieces of wood onto the wagon with tireless concentration. Now and then, she climbed onto the trailer to shift the heap a little further back, hopped down and got straight back into the rhythm. Stoop. Pick up two logs. Throw them onto the trailer. Despite her help, the pile melted away only very slowly, the heap on the trailer could only be seen over the side walls once the shadows of the trees were as long as the field. The sun had long since vanished behind the forest, and only the colour of the sky revealed that it was setting. Liss gave the girl a sign to stop. They uncoupled the saw and pushed it to the edge of the wood. Liss wanted to come back the next day. She turned again, and Sally hooked up the trailer. There was suddenly a fine, white veil hanging between the trees in the forest, and it was properly chilly.

'Civil twilight,' said Sally as she climbed up to her seat. Liss felt those two words release a tension that had lurked unnoticed, deep in her body all day. As if a spring had snapped back. She had her foot on the clutch but didn't engage the gear.

'Civil twilight,' the girl repeated calmly. 'After the sun goes down, you get civil twilight first, then nautical twilight.'

Liss switched the engine off again and turned to Sally.

'Civil twilight: the sun is at one to six degrees below the horizon. There's still no need for artificial light outdoors, barely any stars are visible.'

It's like a poem, thought Liss, as fluent as if she's learnt it by heart.

'Nautical twilight,' Sally continued, and Liss could hear a note of mockery. 'Most stars are visible. The sun is at six to twelve degrees below a straight horizon that is on an imaginary line with the two of us. Unfortunately, there's a forest in the way here.'

'How do you know all that?' asked Liss.

Sally looked at her with a crooked smile.

'If you want to be the best, you need to know things other people don't know. You need to know that in this country, it's not enough for it just to get dark and then light again. Because everything has to be done in an orderly way.'

Liss still didn't quite understand, but it was good that the girl was talking to her. She started the engine. The tractor's nose rose a little before the heavily laden trailer could get moving on the soft forest floor. Sally was holding tightly to the iron backrest with one hand as she leant forwards and raised her voice so that Liss could hear her.

'If the law says that you have to have your headlights on when it's dark, you also have to be able to say when darkness starts. Everything is regulated. Darkness begins with nautical twilight, and you can calculate the start of it for every day. You're not the only one who has a clever father.'

Sally leant back in her seat. Liss looked over to her. The mist was rising up from the fields, a red moon was climbing above the black silhouette of the village, and it was at precisely that moment that the first deer broke out of the forest. Liss saw it and pointed. Sally looked as the second followed it and then, right in front of them, another. Liss looked at Sally, and they both found themselves smiling when, unexpectedly, a fourth leapt after them and crashed into the engine, stumbled and fell and went under the back wheel before the heavy vehicle came to a stop, even though Liss had immediately stamped on the brake.

'Shit!' said Sally, climbing down from the tractor. Liss was already down when the doe screamed. The cry was like a slap. Liss bit her teeth together as she crouched. She'd never run an animal over before. And to do it now, with the tractor.

The animal was trying to get to its feet, but it was lying between the front and back wheel and Liss could see at once that both hind legs were broken, and probably its pelvis too. There was nothing to be done. She saw Sally's face on the other side.

'Shall I pull it out? What ... what do we do now?'

Liss shook her head and stood up.

'There's no point.'

She stopped the engine. The deer screamed again. Liss felt her insides grow calm and cold. She reached under the tractor seat for the tin box held in place by a bungee cord. Sally came over. Liss pointed to the trailer.

'Get the ear defenders. Both sets.'

The girl got onto the drawbar and handed down the ear defenders, which she'd jammed onto the side wall. Liss had opened the case and taken out the pistol. Sally was standing beside her again as she pulled the rubber seal off the cigar box and pushed a cartridge into the magazine.

'Want to...'

She didn't finish the sentence. The doe squealed again and the strangest thing was that the other three deer were standing only a hundred metres away on the field, grazing and simply raising their heads now and then.

It's always the way, thought Liss. In the end, you're always on your own. She took the ear defenders from Sally's hand and put them on. Sally followed suit, hesitantly. Then Liss took the pistol from the seat, pushed in the magazine and pulled the slide back as she crouched down beside the deer.

'Get behind me,' she called to Sally, took the pistol in both hands, exhaled and fired. Despite the ear defenders, the shot echoed deafeningly. At the same moment, all tension fell away from the animal, only the broken hind legs twitched once or twice more.

'Shit,' said Liss, as she pulled the deer out from between the wheels by the foreleg, straightened up and took off the ear defenders. 'Shit.'

'What now?' asked Sally.

Liss could see how messed up she was. She made an effort not to sound gruff. The girl couldn't help the fact that *she* hadn't reacted quickly enough. She could have braked when they saw the first deer, but she hadn't been thinking.

'You won't like it,' she warned quietly. 'You can go on ahead. I have to gut it.'

The girl looked at her, and then at the pistol in her hand. Then she shook her head.

No way. She'd shot the deer, just like that, the way you might take out the bins or have a shower. Just a matter of course. And the shot had been so incredibly loud ... They never sounded like that in films. She'd felt the report in her belly.

'Can you give me a couple of ties?'

Liss handed her the pistol with one hand; with the other, she dragged the deer's body over the track to the edge of the forest. 'And put the pistol back in the case, OK?'

Sally felt the pistol lying heavy and warm in her hand. It was the first time she'd held a real gun. Kind of cool. Kind of awful but cool all the same.

'The ties!'

Liss sounded impatient. Sally hurried to lay the pistol back in the tin box and undo a couple of the thin, rough cords from the handrail, where they always hung. She brought them to Liss, who knelt beside the doe and knotted the first cord around its back leg. Sally hesitated briefly but then knelt too and looped the tie around the other leg. At first it was funny to touch it, but in the end she did.

'Pull,' said Liss briefly, getting to her feet. She pointed to the pine ahead of her, which had two branches growing out of either side of the trunk at about head height. Liss threw her end of the cord over the left-hand branch, and Sally did the same. Then they pulled the deer up. The dull sound of its back hitting the tree trunk was weird, and the doe looked gross, hanging head down from the tree. It was getting properly dark now. Sally shivered. She saw Liss take her penknife from the back pocket of her jeans, open it and calmly cut a single, circular slit between the doe's legs, then cautiously push the knife under the pelt and rip it from top to bottom.

'Whoa!' said Sally, suddenly gagging, but she soon had it back under control. Liss turned to her.

'You mustn't puncture the paunch,' she said, almost apologetically, 'or the meat will be spoiled.' She turned away again. How cool she was about it all. How precise. As if she'd done it a thousand times before. Reluctantly, Sally came closer as Liss positioned the knife again and slit the whitish shimmering silverskin. It sounded shit. It sounded like someone running a pair of scissors through thick cloth. Was that what an operation was like? Did it sound like that when you cut someone's belly open? Now she felt sick.

'What are you doing?' she asked. Her tongue was wading in saliva. Her whole mouth was suddenly full of it.

'Hunters call it gralloching. You have to take the innards out.'

'Why ... why don't we just leave it alone?'

Liss paused for a moment. Her hands were bloody. Was that Liss? The woman was so ... She didn't know why she was so fascinated by how easily Liss could kill, how easily she could cut up the warm animal body, have her hands covered in blood.

'It died needlessly anyway,' she answered calmly, 'it would be an utter waste to leave it. This way, at least we can eat it.'

She had slit the belly and the breast. The animal gaped open and, all at once, against her will, Sally was fascinated. She'd never seen a lung in reality before, or real guts either. Her insides looked pretty similar. She stepped closer.

'Can you hold that?' asked Liss, pointing to the gullet.

Sally reached for it. She didn't want to show weakness and besides ... she wanted to. She wanted to know what it was like. Inside the deer was much less bloody than she'd expected, but obviously ... Liss hadn't shot it in the heart, had she? She was astonished by the feeling of the oesophagus. She'd been expecting something soft, fragile, but in reality it felt like a warm, firm pipe. Liss made a grinding cut into the animal's jaw. Then she stepped back a little.

'You can take the entrails out now. Carefully, so that the paunch doesn't split.'

Sally pulled on the gullet and the innards fell onto the forest floor. They steamed slightly in the cool air. Sally gulped again and again. The doe was no longer bleeding. At the foot of the tree was a small, dark-red spot where the blood pooled and slowly seeped away.

'How do you know all that?' she asked Liss, for something to say. She had never seen an animal butchered before. She had never seen how easy it all was, or how tiny was the moment that lay between life and death. Ten minutes, and the leaping doe had become meat, hanging from the tree, feeling nothing more.

Liss wiped her hands and the knife on the moss, folded it up and pocketed it.

'We'll hide it under the wood. Strictly speaking, we ought to have called the gamekeeper. You and I,' she suddenly smiled at Sally, 'have just been poaching.'

And you've got a pistol under your tractor seat, thought Sally as she helped Liss to throw the deer onto the trailer and stack a few logs on top of it. You've only got a pistol on the tractor.

18 September

Sally was sitting in the hayloft hatch, reading. Liss's house was full of books. Lying around everywhere. Open and face down with broken spines, or with a pencil between the pages, the jacket folded or simply a dry leaf as a bookmark. Not just in the house. In the kitchen, on cupboards and windowsills, in her bike basket and, of course, in the bathroom. Sally had once even found one hanging over a bar in the henhouse when she'd gone to fetch the eggs. An abandoned adventure novel, gathering dust. It was hard to establish what Liss liked; apparently, she read pretty much anything, indiscriminately. Children's books and science fiction, specialist books on machinery or arduous-looking novels. Sally wasn't sure if it was cool or weird. In her family, nobody read. Apart from the newspaper on the iPad or whatever. But here there were so many books, and there was so much time that the books probably came to you of their own accord. Maybe it was because the days here seemed so indeterminately uniform, and because it felt as though she'd been here for a very long time and not just about two weeks.

She was sitting in the hayloft hatch, and the sun was shining on her legs. She liked sitting so high above the farm. The first time Liss had seen her sitting up there, her eyes had rested on her for longer than usual, but she hadn't said anything. No: get down from there it's far too high you'll fall are you mad that's dangerous get down from there get down from there right now get down. Yet she herself had felt a little queasy when she'd discovered the narrow wooden door and opened it for the first time. It was so funny that a door could lead into nothing. Simply into thin air, eight or ten metres up. That first time, she'd lain flat on her belly and looked down. Then she'd turned onto her back and looked up. Over the door, a beam jutted out a metre or so; set into it was a wooden pulley that you could run a rope over. Later, she'd sat on the boards of the hayloft and slowly slid over to the hatch, until she could hang her legs out, over the brink, one hand still holding the doorframe. Her bare heels touched the warm wall. It took her a while to figure out why that felt so good but then, to her surprise, she realised what it was: freedom. It was a sense of freedom, though she didn't actually have a clue why. If she fell, she'd be dead. Or paralysed. And that was very much not the plan, even if they always thought it was. She had no desire to be dead. Or broken. It was the exact opposite. She wanted to be clear, pure, exact, perfect, and that was never possible. But sitting up here, on the boundary between falling and safety, that felt free, and good.

She was sitting in the hayloft hatch, and the sun was shining on her legs, and she was reading. The book was called *The Outsiders of Uskoken Castle*, and at first she'd thought it was a children's book, but it wasn't really. She liked the way the story was told. It didn't seem to need many words at all. The language was as sparse as the landscape in the book. Sally sometimes felt understood when she read about Branko, wanted by nobody. With her, everyone acted like they wanted her, wanted her a lot, but what they really wanted was a mirror image that they could call Sally so they'd be less embarrassed by the fact that they actually only ever looked at themselves and that they'd probably love it best of all if they could only ever fuck themselves so as not to have to get involved with anyone else. Nobody wanted her the way she was, she thought without great emotion, the open book on her legs.

Down below, Liss walked across the yard. She was carrying a couple of wicker baskets, stacked one inside the other, and she vanished into the barn. Sally could hear her below, then she came out again. She was pushing a wheelbarrow with the baskets in it.

'How do you actually make your money?' she called down. 'I mean, how do you earn a living?'

Liss looked up at her. She had to squint against the sun.

'Blackmail,' she answered drily after quite a while. 'And trafficking girls.'

Sally had to laugh. Liss made jokes so rarely that they were always a surprise.

'I'm going to pick pears,' she called up. 'You wanted me to show you some of the varieties. Want to come?'

Sally put the book aside and reached for the rope that she'd attached to the pulley a few days back. Legs around one end of the rope, like in PE. Hands on the other. And then the breathless, magical moment when she slipped off the threshold and hung in the air. Hand over hand, she lowered herself down, slowly revolving on her own axis.

'I don't know whether you noticed,' Liss remarked as she reached the bottom, 'but there's a ladder inside that barn.'

Sally grinned and blew on her hands. It seemed that Liss had her humorous days.

They were in the garden before she remembered that there were only apple trees there. But Liss wasn't stopping. She pushed the barrow round the corner of the machine shed, where the beehives stood, and it was only now that Sally noticed a narrow path there, between the hedge and the back wall of the shed, almost entirely overgrown with elder bushes. The metal wheelbarrow scraped along the plaster. Grooves scored into the pale-grey mortar showed that this wasn't the first time. Just before the other end of the shed, Liss stopped, reached over the barrow and unhooked a garden gate that Sally could barely have made out in the hedge. Liss pushed the wheelbarrow through and had to duck under the branches. Sally followed her and stopped, almost stunned, in the knee-high grass. She'd thought she knew the village around Liss's farm quite well by now. She'd never have believed that an orchard of this size could be hidden behind the neighbouring schoolhouse. And this wasn't just an orchard. It was like a garden in a book. Overgrown. Stinging nettles as tall as a man in the corners. Entirely enclosed by hedges. Full of flowers and weeds. Full of wild, sweet smells.

'Shit,' she said reverently.

'Yes,' answered Liss briefly.

She used the barrow to plough a path through the tall grass to the first of many pear trees, standing in meticulous rows, which looked strange in this wilderness.

'Esperens Herrenbirne,' she said, pointing at the fruit, which didn't really look like pears at all.

'Those aren't pears,' said Sally as she came closer. 'Those are large eggs.'

Liss made a face. Sally couldn't tell whether or not it was a smile.

'That's the lovely thing about nature. It doesn't conform to what we think is right. Even if some people try to force it to grow the way they like it. Belgium. 1831. Have a taste.'

She picked one of the brown-striped, grey-yellow pears from the branch, took a knife from her pocket, cut a piece off and handed it to Sally. It was yellowish, and it felt strangely sweet in her mouth because the grainy flesh melted between her tongue and gums.

Liss took the basket from the wheelbarrow pan, threw it into the grass and halted.

'Come here,' she hissed, suddenly urgent. 'Come and see!'

Sally took a step closer and followed Liss's gaze. She just caught a glimpse of a small snake vanishing into the grass.

'No way!' Sally exclaimed, between shock and fascination. 'Snakes? You've got snakes in your garden?'

'Slowworms. They're actually lizards. And they're not dangerous.'

Then she suddenly laughed.

'What?' Sally asked over her shoulder. She was tracking the lizard, cautious but full of curiosity.

'There's something symbolic about it,' Liss said, bone dry once more. 'I give you a pear off the tree and then a slowworm turns up. I just don't know what it symbolises.'

Sally didn't answer. The slowworm had gone. How nuts was that? She'd never seen a garden like this before. The sun set a swarm of midges dancing and shimmering between the trees.

Liss had walked after her and was now standing by a tree that towered over the others. There was low-hanging fruit within reach, but Liss jumped up a little, grabbed a branch and swung herself, pretty skilfully, into the tree, rapidly climbed two or three metres and then plucked a pear from the sunlit crown.

'Here,' she said, throwing it to Sally.

It was another of those moments. Sally didn't know any adults who just climbed trees like that. She knew adults who exercised. But it was all about sport. A serious business. It wasn't movement to get somewhere. It was movement to be something. Slimmer or faster or better. When really, they were just going round in one big circle.

She'd just picked up the pear when something glinted beside her as it fell, then there was the knife stuck in the ground, not half a metre from her shoes.

As she climbed down, Liss said: 'Cut it through the middle.'

The fruit was heavy and warm from the sun. Sally bent, pulled the knife out of the ground and wiped it on her bare legs. Then she cut through the pear.

'Wow,' she said.

It was like opening up a rare flower. The seeds lay gleaming black-brown in bright-red chambers. Around them, like a bed, was white flesh, surrounded in turn by a rose-red bell. A slender white dash ran down from the stem, dividing it. And it was all inside a thin, warm, reddish-brown shell.

'I've never seen anything like it,' said Sally.

'A blood pear,' said Liss, once she was back on the ground. 'Nobody knows how long they've been around. Try.'

Sally cut off a larger piece this time. She wanted to taste the red and the white. It was hard to find a word for the way this pear felt in her mouth – firm yet melting. And she thought the red tasted sweeter and that there was a tiny trace of bitterness in the white, and that together it was a taste that ... maybe sunlight would taste like that after a long summer, if it fell through the distant blue of the sky and then the ancient green of tall trees, and landed right on your tongue.

'Want some?' she asked, offering Liss half.

She shook her head. 'I prefer others.'

She walked to another tree, hung with long, very green pears.

'Those aren't ripe yet, are they?'

Liss picked one, bit off the stalk and spat it out.

'Bosc pear. An accidental cross. Discovered in the forest in Apremont, sometime during the French Revolution. Some people call it the Kaiser Alexander pear.'

She held it out to Sally. She bit a piece off. This time the flesh was firm and the taste was tart.

'I like them when they're not quite ripe,' said Liss.

'How do you know all this?' asked Sally. She ran her hand over the stinging nettles. Sometimes she liked the burning on her palms. 'About the forest and the dates and all that stuff.'

Liss took another bite from the pear, then she flung out her arm and hurled the rest over the hedge.

'I learnt it all by heart.'

She went back to the wheelbarrow to fetch one of the baskets.

'Or, to be precise, I had to learn it all by heart. Every tree, every pear, every name.'

In passing, she plucked a pear off another tree and threw it to Sally without looking. Sally caught it. It looked like something from an old picture. Sally had never seen a pear like that in any supermarket. Red, glowing flames licked over the sunward side, fading through orange into yellow on the other side. It was a very large, heavy, almost exotically irregular pear.

'Margarete Marillat.' Liss was almost singing now, a derisive drone. 'A French variety. The very latest thing, when I was thirteen. A show fruit. Looks much better than it tastes. And it goes bad quickly.'

Sally leant against the tree beside her. The rough bark on her back felt good, even through her thin T-shirt.

'Who made you learn that by heart?' she asked.

'The previous owner,' answered Liss, starting to pick the Marillat pears. She threw them carelessly into the basket.

'Won't they bruise?' asked Sally, peeling herself away from the trunk to help.

'They'll just get pressed anyway. They don't even make good schnapps. They're only good for juicing. But it doesn't matter with the others either. We don't eat them. They're for the mash.'

They worked in silence. The garden was full of the humming of bees and the September light and the scent of the pears.

‘The previous owner was your father, wasn’t he?’

Liss didn’t answer at first. The pears were so big that the basket soon filled, even though they hadn’t brought a ladder. Sally watched Liss as she worked. Quick, but not the way she’d been with the potatoes. Here, she was working furiously and not as evenly. Once the basket was overflowing, Liss heaved it onto the wheelbarrow in one single rapid explosion of strength, without giving Sally a chance to help.

‘He was an arsehole,’ she said, between two hasty breaths. ‘That’s all. If he was a father ... nobody needs one like that.’

She walked to the hedge, where there was a ladder that Sally had only just noticed. Liss pulled it out of the bushes and leant it against a trunk, between the branches.

‘Want to go up?’

Sally nodded and climbed the ladder, then positioned herself wide-legged, with one foot on each of two diverging branches, leant her back against the trunk, and found that she could easily reach up into the crown from there. The fruit hung gleaming and beautiful between the leaves. Rhythmically, she threw pear after pear down to Liss. She took a little time before asking what she wanted to know.

‘Did he hit you?’

Pear off the branch. Pear dropping into Liss’s hands.

‘Didn’t have to.’

Pear in the basket.

‘Everything had to be exact. Perfectly exact. Perfectly orderly. I still remember the way he planted the trees. He laid out rectangular batter boards, like for building a house. A tree every five metres longways, a tree every four metres crossways. There were grids like that all over the place, even if you couldn’t see them. On the farm and in the village and in my room once I finally had one, and even after I'd turned sixteen or seventeen or eighteen. Especially then.'

It was good that she was up the tree just then, thought Sally. It was the first time Liss had spoken about herself. She climbed another two branches higher, to get to the highest fruit.

'Reading was out of order. Listening to music was out of order. Leaving things as they are was right out of order. You can tie trees to a stake to make them grow straight. All his life he thought you could do that to people too.'

The second basket was full now too, but there were still lots of pears in the crown. Liss fetched another. Sally waited, her back against the trunk, her legs stretched, straddling two branches, her face in the sun.

When Liss put the basket in the grass, she asked: 'When did he die?'

Liss looked up at her.

'He's not dead,' she said, her voice cold. 'He moved away. Along with his wife, who spent her whole life with him in squares. That's why I only go into his orchard once a year. Only for the harvest. Because otherwise I feel bad about the pears.'

Sally had picked and thrown down most of the pears. There were only a few on the very outside branches that she couldn't reach. She climbed down, hung from a branch and let herself drop the rest of the way. She wiped her hands on her shorts. Then she looked at Liss.

'This is the most beautiful garden I've ever seen in all my life. I mean, I understand that it ... that you ... that it used to be ... different. That to you it's...' She was hunting for words. Liss said nothing as she bent to pick up a few pears that had fallen in the grass. The right word came to Sally.

'I can see that the garden used to be a cage to you. But look what it's turned into!'

She spun in a circle, trying to encompass it all. The weathered fence panels, pressed gently inwards by the wildly overgrown hedges. The parallel grid of trees, with fanned-out crowns, slanted trunks and clouds of leaves that reduced all the right angles to fading memories. The sea of grass, straggly weeds and stinging nettles, through which the light September breeze sent pale-green waves rippling from one end of the orchard to the other.

'It's all...' Again she sought out the right word. 'It's all like a wonderful punishment for trying to force growing things into a mould. Don't you see that?'

Sally had the sudden feeling of having discovered something and desperately wanted Liss to understand it too.

'By never going into the orchard, letting everything just grow, leaving everything in peace, you've made it magical...'

That last word had just slipped out. She hadn't meant to say it, it sounded so clichéd. But it was said now.

'You have to take it back,' she added, because Liss was showing no reaction. 'It belongs to you now.'

Liss grabbed the handles of the wheelbarrow, where she'd now put the second basket too.

'Open the gate for me,' she said.

It was hard to pull the garden gate over the tall weeds. Sally tugged hard on the latch, stumbled backwards and fell into the grass because she'd ripped the screws right out of the rotten wood.

'You see,' she laughed, 'now you can't even close it again!'

Liss's features relaxed, and Sally could see a smile playing around the corners of her lips.

'I've never ... I'd never seen it like that,' she said thoughtfully.

Much later, when the baskets of pears had been decanted into sacks, when the sacks had gradually covered the entire trailer floor, and Liss had started the tractor and told Sally to get up, she called out 'thank you' without looking at her, over the noise of the diesel engine springing slowly into life.

19 September

Gone out.

Liss put a foot on the chair, and rested her elbows on her knee and her chin in her hand, as she laid the slip of paper back on the kitchen table. It was the first time the girl had left her a note. Previously she'd been there or not, or gone up in the barn, without saying anything.

Liss tried to think, but thinking about feelings didn't work; you *had* feelings. Sometimes more than one at the same time. Like now. The note was saying: I want you to know something about me. I'm not indifferent to what you think.

Liss didn't know whether she wanted that. The torn-off corner of the newspaper, the pencil scribble in the thoroughly ungirly handwriting were also saying: I'm a thread that the girl has spun between the two of you, without asking. As fine as a cobweb, yet you feel a tug on it. One thread becomes threads and threads become cords and cords are woven into a net.

Liss straightened up, took the note and threw it into the cold kitchen stove.

Almost three weeks she's been here now, she thought, and again she had two contradictory emotions that were hard to pigeonhole because she didn't have the right words and things had probably always been that way.

A January morning, of blue cold. The grapevines numbed with black frost. The stream in the valley steaming with mist. A barge heaped with coal trekked silently upstream, the water parting lethargically, as if it were thick with the cold. On the other side of the valley, the sun stood red over the hills.

She waited, the heavy rucksack in grey-green canvas on her shoulders. She didn't need to take it off. She was strong. She could hike all day with it on her back, if necessary. She'd taken it from the storeroom where he kept his army stuff. Years ago, when she'd been fourteen, she'd had the locksmith make a duplicate key. He didn't know that she knew all his keys, all his hiding places in the kitchen drawer among the sealing rings and in the beams above the little window in the pigsty, and on a string in the cistern in the upstairs loo. She smiled bitterly. If you're often locked in, you start to think in keys.

The rucksack felt good and heavy on her shoulders. No more, she thought. Nobody's locking me in anymore. She hadn't run away. She'd told him. She had walked into the kitchen where they were sitting, drinking the thin coffee with the milk skin that she hated so much. He smells like an old man, she'd thought, as she stepped into the kitchen, not even sixty, and he already smells like an old man.

I'm leaving.

Nobody leaves, he'd said. Then he was standing up, then the cup was in pieces and the coffee was dripping down the wall over the stove, and he was shouting. Nobody leaves. Nobody leaves.

And she'd picked up his rucksack, so he could see it. Had picked up the rucksack and said: That's true. You two don't.

Then she'd gone, and he'd followed her, and in the hallway he'd tried to pull her by the arm. She'd turned around and noticed for the first time that she was taller than him. Only a little, but taller, and she'd felt as though she'd leant down to him as she said quietly, very close to his face: I'm leaving, old man. You're not locking me in any longer.

Up the hill.

She hadn't needed to tell Sonny anything else. He always picked her up there. Up in the vineyard, where she'd taken his hand the first time, and he'd been so surprised that she'd almost let go again. But today wasn't always. Today was for always.

She could already hear the unmistakable soft rattle of the VW engine, even though Sonny's camper must still be way down in the valley, out of sight. A warmth spread through her stomach, dissolving the slight nausea that was there every morning she woke up in the house. Sonny.

She watched the camper as it crawled up the track between the vineyards. Good job there was no snow on the ground. Sonny didn't have winter tyres on. But there'd be no snow on the ground in Italy, or in the south of France, or in Spain. They'd get over the Alps somehow or other. She'd never been in the Alps, but they'd manage it. Sonny and her.

The sound of the engine grew louder, the camper climbed up to her, came purring to a stop. She opened the side door and threw her rucksack in. Sonny turned to her.

Eight o'clock. You said eight o'clock.

She was a little surprised.

Nice to see you, too. I couldn't bear it at home any longer. And I didn't mind waiting.

I'd have come sooner, but you said eight.

She threw the sliding door shut and climbed forward into the passenger seat.

Italy, she said. Are you pleased?

Sonny turned. He laid his arm on the passenger seat as he twisted round to do so.

Yes. He pulled away. I really could've been here sooner, but you said eight.

She wound down the window. A touch of the nausea from earlier was back again. She breathed in deeply. The air was cold but fresh.

In Spain, she called out to Sonny through the wind rushing past the open window, they're harvesting the oranges now.

Sonny smiled slightly.

Then open the window again in Spain, he shouted back, it's cold here.

Finally, they turned off onto the motorway.

She looked out. It was pouring with rain, and she'd been able to see her breath when she'd walked across the yard earlier. A day that was pre-empting November. The girl would get wet. As far as she knew, she didn't have a raincoat.

She shook her head and reached for the tobacco pouch on the shelf over the stove. It was at least two weeks since she'd smoked, but she felt like it today. She rolled the cigarette standing up, put the pouch back and lit a match. Then she opened the glass door onto the yard, looked into the rain, smoked and tried not to think at all. On the road, old Anni was riding up to the church on her bike, head bent; she didn't see her because she was wearing a plastic cape made from an old fertiliser sack. A sudden sense of affection for that robust old woman washed through her like a warm little wave.

Rain. Smoke. Rain. She'd always liked watching the rain, listening to the rain and smoking; in the old days, sitting in the window at night once everyone else was finally asleep.

It had been a hundred years ago.

She threw the cigarette into the rain and went down into the cellar to check on the mash.

Even from the stone steps down into the cellar, she was hit by the overwhelming smell of fermenting pears. For two days, they'd harvested pears, passed hundreds of kilos through the fruit mill and then pureed them. Liss had to smile as she remembered Sally's face the first time she'd seen the stick blender: Huh? That's not a blender, that's a power drill. Sally had enjoyed heaving the blender into the barrels, holding it with both hands and fighting the heavy mass of pears, weighing out the yeast and the sugar, and stirring them in. Liss had watched her tipping the barrels with her slender arms to twist them out of the way. It hadn't looked as though she'd never done anything like that before. She'd generally had to show harvest hands how to do such things. The girl often knew where to take hold of a thing before you told her.

Liss inspected the barrels, checking whether the airlocks were seated correctly and were properly filled. She added dilute sulphuric acid to two of them. The whisper of the fermentation gases in the glass tubes mingled with the equally quiet rushing of the rain that she could hear through the half-open cellar windows. Liss stopped still. It was often surprisingly bright down here because the windows were well positioned, but the light that day was dull, and the long passageway that ran under the yard to the barn looked dark and unfriendly. She shrugged. It was a day when you couldn't do much. The fields were sodden. The forest was wet. On days like this, she had been known to read from morning till night.

She took the wooden staircase at the other end of the cellar and lingered a while in the barn. She saw that her bike was still there. Sally had taken the other one. She stood in the door and looked into the rain. Maybe she should imitate the girl. Maybe you could spend half a day acting like your own life had nothing to do with you.

Determinedly, she strode across the yard to fetch a jacket, not avoiding a single puddle. It was good to feel the water splash up.

Sally was dripping. She'd wrapped her jumper in a plastic bag and jammed it onto the pannier rack, but everything else was soaked. She stood up on the pedals and kept a slow, steady pace. Her calves were burning, but they had been for quarter of an hour, and it was good not to give in. You could always do more than you thought, always. The hill dragged on, but there was no wind and the rain cooled her off. It was good to be alone outside. The bicycle was good. She'd got used to it by now, and it rode really well. She'd taken the narrow track that ascended between the vineyards. It was steeper than the lane. It took her a while to realise that it was the track where she'd first met Liss.

Ride out of the saddle. Don't give in.

Still keeping an even pace, but breathing ever harder, she threw the handlebars from side to side, pulling up on the bars with every stroke, with all her strength, trying to get all her weight and more through the pedals. She found herself thinking about the potatoes that she hadn't kept picking that first time. When she'd just jacked it all in. The memory burnt hot through her belly. Don't give in. Change gears. Ride out of the saddle.

The dripping vines moved past her very slowly. She could see them out of the corners of her eyes. The track below her. Four turns of the crank for every concrete slab. Eight strokes. You could feel each gap between them in the wheels. Clack, clack. Eight strokes. Clack, clack.

'Fuck!' she screamed breathlessly. 'Fuck.' But it wasn't a furious curse, it was simply a shout of exertion, assertive, driving herself on; or maybe it *was* furious, but laden with positive fury, the kind that makes you strong.

She gasped, riding in the smallest gear now, but she didn't give up. Eleven strokes for every concrete slab now. Clack. Clack. It wasn't far now, the ridge was ahead of her. Clack, clack.

When she reached the top, she rode on another three, four metres, before stopping, right out of breath; laid her head on her arms for a moment, exhausted; and felt the blood flow back into her calves as they relaxed. Then she straightened up, stretched her back and looked down. The river lay grey and heavy in the valley. Above it, despite the rain, hung a fine mist. She licked the rain off her upper lip. Her breathing calmed. The wind turbines stood motionless. Was today the first day of autumn? It was strange that, after the last hour, which had been solely movement, exertion to the edge of exhaustion, after that breathless morning she suddenly wanted to stand so still.

No movement.

But yes.

It was as if she could feel the Earth carrying her off. She and the vineyard and the river and the turbines and the entire greyish-bright, rain-soaked landscape. She spread her arms out a little, the bike still between her legs, let the rain fall on her and the drips run down her face. Why didn't they do this stuff in the clinics? In the clinics, they had pouring rain on CDs and you sat around in circles of chairs and were meant to shut your eyes and imagine being out in the rain. *They* were sick. Not her.

Gradually, she started to cool off. The rain was still pleasant, but she needed to move again.

Another minute or two. It was so rare for things to be in

balance. Without either happiness or sorrow. Or, to put it another way: happiness and sorrowfulness in one, in such a state of limbo, in such a perfect balance that you didn't want to move. Maybe that was how tightrope dancers felt when they were that high up, in the one moment when a straight line ran through the very centre of their body and through the very soul of the rope and down to the ground and then into the Earth's innermost core; in that one motionless moment of centredness.

I'm not going into another clinic. I'm not anorexic. I'm not sick!

Sally was yelling. She didn't actually want to yell because she knew that it only made everything worse, but she was still yelling. As if she'd be understood better if she raised her voice.

They were in the living room. Since they'd moved into the new house – another new place – the living room had been the room that made it clearest to her that she and her mother lived in two worlds that just happened to touch at the edges. Tasteful. That word was everywhere, an invisible label hanging from vases and stuck to the bottom of the carpet, on the back of the leather sofa that her mother was currently sitting on, next to the modern paintings on the wall and the waist-height wooden sculptures. It was etched invisibly into the oversized windowpanes, which looked out onto the useless garden with the Japanese ornamental cherry and the blood-red acer. A perfect combination, intended to add a dash of colour to the pocket handkerchief lawn in spring and autumn alike. It wasn't there on her mother's brow. It wouldn't have been necessary. The worst thing was, she didn't do it on purpose. Perhaps it was in her nature to be tasteful and elegant and sophisticated. Sally didn't know. She only knew that she wasn't like that. When she stood in this living room, like now, she felt a stranger to herself.

Her father was sitting on the windowsill. It was as though they were both being very careful not to stand, so as not to give her any feeling of inferiority, of helplessness. Even though she already knew perfectly well that something wasn't right, seeing that her father had come to the house, and it wasn't Christmas or her birthday. He had turned towards her, his hands folded between his knees, almost humble.

We think you are, Sarah.

She just couldn't believe the way they could still run her life, send her away, have her looked for and fetched back. It wasn't even that they hated her or anything. But they just couldn't put up with her any longer. How was it possible to be the child of parents who were just wrong for you, right from the start?

She grimaced with a sudden, malicious thought. Of course. They'd mistaken her for somebody else on the maternity ward. And then when they'd found out a year or two later and told her parents, Papa would definitely have sued them. Because that kind of thing didn't happen to him. Not to him. She could have been clearly not his – black, or Chinese maybe – she grinned to herself, and he'd still have kept her.

Her father was speaking quickly, understandingly, lovingly. It was difficult to resist that voice and, when she'd been little, she'd loved it when he talked like that to her. She'd felt bigger, taken seriously. Today she knew that he always used that voice when he wanted to get something done. She'd bet her mother had fallen for that voice, once upon a time, and for all her rage, she'd almost laughed. She guessed that made two of them, Mama and her.

You're self-harming. You aren't eating. You go running till you almost keel over. That might seem normal to you, but it isn't. It really isn't.

Who says I'm not eating?

Her mother looked up at her. Sad eyes. Now that was something *she* was pretty good at. Papa's soft voice. Mama's sad eyes. Her parents were a dream team. But sadly, only for a dream daughter. Not for her.

I'm just thin. Maybe you can't get this into your heads, but some people are fat and some people are thin. I'm thin. I'm not sick.

You self-harm, her father reminded her. Soft voice. A touch of sorrow. Sometimes Sally thought the two of them were learning from each other when it came to her.

Why are you self-harming? Why aren't you eating. You don't know.

It's part of the illness.

Her mother did stand up now.

It's part of the illness that you can't see that you need help.

Sally couldn't help it. She shouted. The living room needed you to shout in it.

I'm not self-harming. I cut myself. There's a difference. And I do it because it feels right. I'll stop when it stops feeling right, OK? It won't kill me. Other people get tattoos. Or smoke. Or drink. I don't do drugs, I don't smoke, I don't drink. I exercise. I'm not going to mess myself up and mainly: I'm not going into another clinic.

We don't want you to collapse. You're chasing an ideal that—

Sally interrupted him incredulously. She was so surprised that she spoke in an almost normal voice.

Do you guys think I'm thin because I want to be beautiful? Do you really think that? Don't you understand ... that it's... She was searching for words. Then she stretched out an arm and turned slowly in a circle, to take in everything that there was. The living room and her parents and the whole house, the city and her whole life.

She whispered.

The only reason I don't eat is that nothing can taste good here.

♠

Sally grinned, and before she could fall off balance, she raised herself up on the pedals and rode.

She paused briefly where the track came out onto the country road. In the distance, she could make out the contours of the village church through the rain, blurry and grey. She didn't actually want to go back yet, but she was gradually getting cold and she'd already done over thirty kilometres.

It was no fun riding on the lane in this weather. The water pooled in the ruts and made her wheels sluggish, but if she rode further into the middle of the road, the cars passed her so close that she could feel the slipstream, on top of which she was soaked every time by a dirty cloud of spray, thrown up by the wheels. It shouldn't bother her, seeing as she was wet anyway, but the inconsiderate way they all overtook was just so annoying.

'Arsehole!' she screamed after a black Mercedes that passed so near her she swayed in the turbulence and had to grip the handlebars. She stuck her middle finger up, even though there was no way the driver would be able to see her through the spray. On the opposite side of the road, a VW camper braked.

'What?' Sally yelled furiously at the driver, giving him the finger too. The window was wound down and there was a second's delay before Sally recognised Liss. She smiled slightly.

'Want a lift?'

'Is this yours?' asked Sally once they'd stowed the bike inside it. The middle row of seats had been taken out so there was loads of room. Sally had taken her T-shirt off and swapped it for the dry jumper from her plastic bag. She'd kept her wet trousers on. They'd dry by themselves anyway.

'The camper belongs to Gerhard. The man with the big house with the slate roof behind the church. He sometimes needs a tractor, so I let him use mine. And in return, I get to take this. He's got another car anyway.'

Somehow, Sally had always thought Liss had no friends at all. She hadn't seen any visitors since she'd been staying with her.

'Uh-huh,' she said.

Liss gave her a brief glance that she couldn't interpret.

'What?' Sally asked loudly. 'What?'

'You think I don't like people much.'

It wasn't a question. It was a statement. Sally felt seen through. She didn't like the feeling, especially because other people always went and thought they knew everything about her just because they'd got something right for once.

'It's not so hard to guess, is it?' she retorted. 'Where are you going anyway?'

Liss didn't answer right away. Despite the rain, she was driving fast and not at all like someone who only borrowed a car occasionally. Eventually they turned onto a road that led down to the river. Sally could see a solitary barge, chugging through the grey. It was an image that spoke to her somehow. She didn't know exactly what it was saying, but it spoke to her. In the city where she lived, there was no particularly big river. In the city where she lived, nothing large could move.

As they arrived in the valley, Liss turned off again, and now they were following the river upstream, parallel to the water. To their right, the vineyards climbed, sometimes steeply, sometimes more gently. Sally opened the window on her side. The wind spat the smell of rain and greenery into her face.

'To an ossuary,' Liss said loudly. Sally didn't understand.

'What?'

'We're driving to an ossuary.'

Sally shut the window.

'Oh, thanks. That's helpful,' she snarked back. 'I have no idea what an ossuary is.'

Liss twisted her lips into a thin smile.

'I think you might like it. We're nearly there.'

Sally didn't answer, but wound the window down again, leant out and held her face to the headwind. She'd always liked doing that. Liked how it made it hard to breathe. Liked the way air suddenly had weight: if you didn't turn away, it became an invisible fist, soft yet firm, that punched you in the mouth and lungs.

They reached the pukeworthy outskirts of a small town: ugly petrol stations, ugly DIY store, ugly supermarket. But Liss turned off again and they drove up a steep hill, and then suddenly through a gate and over cobblestones, up and up on ever narrower lanes. They stopped on a small square. Liss got out without waiting for Sally. She didn't turn around and left the camper unlocked. It was almost as though she were in a hurry all of a sudden. Sally slipped off her seat, slammed the passenger door and followed her. The cobbles shone dull and grey. All the houses around the square were on the wonk. One of them had sunk so much over the centuries that the half-timbered crossbeam on the right of the house was almost half a metre lower than on the left. Probably people had kept having to change the windows – it looked as though the row of them shrank from left to right. Sally had to grin. How did you live in a house like that, where the ceiling at one end was fifty centimetres lower than at the other? You probably had to nail down the tables and cupboards on the first floor, like on a ship, to stop them sliding towards the righthand wall. It must be really dire to come home drunk to a house like that. You'd probably keel over right on the doorstep. But maybe there were times when it was just funny.

They'd stopped. Liss was waiting on the other side of the square, at the mouth of a little alleyway leading further uphill, but she didn't walk on until she saw that Sally was following her. It was only after a hundred metres or so, when the little lane widened out again into another square, that Sally saw the church. It was far too big for such a small place.

'A church?' she called, disappointed. 'That's it?'

'Come on.'

Liss walked past the church towards a gate in the churchyard wall. Sally caught up with her, but her expectations were suddenly muted. What? she asked herself in the silence. What? And as she walked behind Liss, she realised that it was because she expected more of her than just a church. Not that she gave a shit. If the woman was a fan of a dog kennel, that was fine by her. Nobody else had to like it. But Liss had said that Sally might like what she wanted to show her.

Yeah, great. So now she was expecting Liss to really know her tastes? Why did she keep falling for it? People weren't like that. Everyone was alone. Nobody really understood anyone else. So why should this woman suddenly get it? After three weeks?

'In here,' said Liss. She bent and walked through a low, doorless entrance into a kind of chapel that was leaning against the church wall, but apparently built deeper into the hillside.

OK, not a church. A chapel. Sally couldn't help it, she was still disappointed as she followed her into the windowless passage.

Liss switched on the light and Sally involuntarily caught her breath. She was facing a wall of skulls. A proper wall. At least three metres high and ten metres long. A thousand empty eye sockets were looking at her. A wall of holes where there'd once been noses. A wall of a thousand soundless smiles.

Row upon row of skulls were stacked between layers of ... What were they ... thigh bones? There must be tens of thousands. And it was only now that she noticed that the pillars of the arches to her right and left were ... They were made of thigh bones too. But overlapping like brickwork. The pillars were built out of bones. The arches too. And then that wall of skulls ... She knew it would probably sound stupid, but she couldn't help it, she had to ask.

'They're real, aren't they?'

Liss nodded. 'It's an ossuary. A charnel house. When there's no more room in the graveyard and the graves have to be vacated, they bring the bones here. You can't just throw them away.'

Nothing like that had ever even occurred to Sally before.

'But there are so many,' she whispered.

She couldn't hold back. The thousands upon thousands of bones exerted a strange fascination. She took a few steps forward and touched one of the skulls. Smooth. As if it had been polished. Sally suddenly thought of how often she'd touched somebody else's head, but never without skin and hair. She grasped her own. Felt the warmth. She laid her other hand on the skull. Cold. That was it. That was how far you were from death. Arm's length. She heard Liss laugh quietly.

'What?' she asked, but without any aggression.

'I did that exact thing the first time I was here,' said Liss.

Sally stroked the skull then stepped back and assimilated the image.

'How many are there?'

Liss joined her. 'About twenty thousand.'

'But why ... Who does that? Builds ... builds a wall of bones. Layers them up like...' She didn't know what she was trying to say.

'Better than throwing them all on a heap, I reckon.'

Sally didn't answer. Maybe Liss was right. She walked along the wall, running her finger smoothly along the bones and skulls. When it caught in an eye socket, she suddenly remembered a scene in a boring play they'd read at school. With the prince holding the skull in his hand and droning on about death. If *that* had felt like this ... then. OK, then ... it wasn't boring. You couldn't do anything else after feeling something like this.

The light went out.

'Wait,' said Liss. She heard her feeling for the switch, shut her eyes and laid both hands on the cold wall of bones. What a wild feeling.

'Why do you come here?' she asked, eyelids still shut.

The light went back on. She stared into the empty eyes of a lost face and waited, without turning round. And noticed that Liss was hesitating.

'Have you ever been in love?' she asked slowly.

A hot emotion rose up in Sally, but it was as though it immediately ebbed away through her hands into the cool skulls, leaving nothing behind but a strangely chilled curiosity.

'What kind of a shitty question is that?' she answered, almost calmly. 'Of course I've been in love.' She emphasised the *in love* as if it were meant ironically, which it wasn't. 'And it's none of your business.'

'No,' said Liss, 'I know that.'

She stepped up to Sally and also touched one of the skulls with her fingertips. Very gently, she traced the contours. Sally shoved her hands in the pockets of her still-clammy trousers.

'Well,' said Liss in an almost light-hearted tone, 'at any rate, I was in love the first time I came here. I was a bit older than you, twenty maybe.'

'Who was it?' Sally asked. 'The guy with the bike?'

'And that's none of *your* business,' Liss answered impersonally. 'At any rate, I was unlucky in love. Very unlucky. At that time, I hitchhiked a lot. So I ended up here by chance one day. I didn't want to go into the church either, by the way,' she added with a very slight smile. 'But I've always liked churchyards. That's how I found the ossuary. On an incredibly hot June day.'

She fell silent suddenly. Perhaps she had the feeling that she'd already said too much. Sally knew that one. It really was always better not to tell people anything. Liss put her hands in her pockets now too, leant back, relaxed, on the wall of bones and turned to her.

'And then coming here, full of unhappiness and romantic fantasies of what it would be like if you were suddenly dead because you'd jumped off a bridge or had an accident or only had six weeks to live – all the stuff people imagine to force other people to love them in return.'

Sally suddenly felt strangely as though someone had caught her doing something forbidden.

'Then standing here, facing twenty thousand dismembered skeletons, facing this wall of skulls that's so weirdly beautiful, you suddenly know that your so-called unhappiness doesn't mean a thing. That, actually, nothing really means anything at all, because everything passes.'

The light went off again. This time it was Sally who looked for the switch. It gave her time to find the right words for the furious emotion that had found its way into her mouth and wanted to get out. She felt along the wall for it. Then she turned to Liss who was still leaning on the wall of bones.

'What a load of shit,' she said very loudly. Her voice echoed a little in the ossuary. 'What a massive pile of shit. There's no way you're that empty. I know people who're that empty, totally empty. People like that ... honestly, I know enough of them. But what you're saying there, that's just a huge pile of shit. Everything means something. Just because you'll be dead one day, that doesn't mean...' She was lost for words.

Liss said nothing.

'What?' cried Sally, in a similar fury to the one she'd felt earlier while cycling – that good fury that drove you on. 'What? Just because one day you'll be just ... bones,' she pointed to the wall, 'you reckon that makes you dead inside before that? That's not you. Not you. That's just a load of shit what you're saying.'

She turned and walked out of the ossuary into the rain. It was quite a while till Liss came after her, but Sally didn't walk away. She stopped when Liss came to stand beside her in the rain.

'That's how it felt back then,' she said calmly. 'It's a good place for me.'

Sally needed a little time. It was kind of true. It was a good place. But what Liss had said didn't fit with it. And it didn't fit with Liss. But she didn't know how she could say that without sounding stupid.

'Here,' she said spontaneously, turning around and pressing her rain-wet hand onto her brow. 'Here. You're warm. Warm, get that?'

It wasn't until she took her hand away again that she realised it was the first time in three weeks they'd touched each other. They'd never taken the other's hand or anything. Sally inhaled deeply.

'Yes,' Liss suddenly replied, loudly and in a surprisingly light tone, 'it's OK, I've got it.'

She smiled a little and Sally sighed with relief.

'Café or church?' she asked.

'The deer,' Sally answered very firmly, 'let's drive home and you can show me how you prepare the deer.' Home, thought Liss. She said 'home'.

Up the old tower in the ruined castle above the town. The door was actually blocked, nailed shut, because the steps were unsafe. Sonny had broken it open the first time they'd been there.

Sonny! What if somebody comes?

Nobody'll come, he'd laughed. She had to laugh too because he was so carefree. In the motorbike panniers, he had a crowbar; it made such short work of the bolt that the screws went flying. And then he shoved it under the wooden door and skilfully jemmied it right off its hinges.

We'll put it back later. This can be our tower.

Our tower. How wonderful that had sounded. Around them was nothing but the castle's ruined walls, and down there was the well; a maid had been thrown down it during the Thirty Years' War, to poison it. Every time she stood there, she found herself imagining that. If you threw ten pfennigs into a machine there, the light in the well went on for two minutes. There was a thick iron grid over the top, through which you could see down into the depths. The water glittered a very long way down. There was a cup chained to the edge; you could use it to scoop up water from a little basin and then pour it down the well. The falling water looked beautiful. It fell and fell, and after a while you heard it hit, and the black surface of the water there below suddenly rippled silver. What would it be like to fall that far?

Our tower. An early summer day under a wind-tattered, gloomy sky, the first time they'd stood up there together. It had been such a strange, tingly feeling to be in the middle of an autumn day, yet to know that it wasn't winter on its way but summer. The wind was cold and rough in their hair, but they enjoyed its coarse tenderness. Round here it was rare for the wind to blow really hard. On an impulse, she jumped onto the tower's broad wall.

Hey!

Sonny came over, wanted to hold on to her legs.

Don't. I can stand better alone.

The whole countryside below her, and she was like a queen over the depths. Seen from up here, their village almost vanished among the fields.

You look hot, standing up there.

When he said stuff like that it really was like a sudden heat shooting through her body. He thought she was hot.

She jumped off the wall. There he stood. Easy-going, his long hair tousled by the wind too.

You think?

He nodded.

Very hot, even.

She let him pull her to him and felt his mouth on hers, always a bit rough, like the wind, but full of energy and desire.

I wrote you a song.

Now he was out of breath too.

Really?

He'd hidden the guitar up here on the tower. He'd been that certain she'd come here with him.

Arrogant bastard.

She gave him a playful slap. He laughed and held her hand tight.

That's what you like about me though.

And you? What do you like about yourself?

Money and possessions, he laughed. He picked up the guitar. Now listen up.

She sat cross-legged on the wall. At her back was forty-five metres of nothing. In front of her was Sonny, tuning the guitar with a few deft movements. Around her was the wind, setting the tattered flags rattling. It must be unusual for the old fabric to be moved so fast and so hard. Liss had to smile. Rip it to shreds, she thought. 'There swirls the storm, a rearranger...'

Then Sonny sang. His voice, which she loved so much, was rough and sounded like yearning as he began.

Come a long way, looking for you, heading up north, searching for you...

The wind was suddenly cold as the notes went through Liss, and she recognised what he was singing.

Pretty. Does Caro know that you're singing that to me?

Sonny stopped.

What?

You wrote that for me? Huh? For me? Hmm ... Well, at least you're playing it live for me: you only taped it for Caro.

Liss!

No.

She picked up her denim jacket and headed for the steps.

Liss, bloody hell, you *know* that Caro ... that it's been over for ages. I was thinking of you when I wrote the song. Honest. Even then, I was thinking of you.

Bullshit.

Liss!

She ran down the stairs, hot with rage at her own stupidity. Hot with shame and hot with the pointless wish for what Sonny had said to be true, that he really had been thinking about her even then. She ran across the grass in the castle courtyard without turning around, and thought about the well. So that was what it felt like to fall forever.

22 September

Sally had written the letter. She'd cycled to the town, bought a stamp from the machine there and then posted it a couple of villages further on. Hello don't worry I'm staying with a friend for a while no need to look for me it's fine. The kind of stuff you write when you don't want to write at all. Writing the word friend had been strange.

But it gave her a funny feeling all the same. She'd been here for over three weeks now. Nothing special, actually. She'd been away for much longer and had never written a letter. The summer camps that she hadn't liked. Nearly every year. Since she was twelve. And then the clinics, most of which weren't called that, but health centres or rehabilitation centres or whatever. Then it had been six or eight weeks and she hadn't written, even though you sometimes weren't allowed a mobile phone at the start, and she hadn't felt like phoning. The funny feeling was different.

She was in the pear orchard, thinking. The morning was the kind she liked. Others always wanted it to be hot and sunny. She liked it when it was windy and cool; just cool enough that you could feel the wind on your skin without shivering. And today the wind was strong. It moved the crowns of the pear trees even though most of them weren't very tall and they were sheltered by the wall of the engine shed. The fluctuating sunlight came and went rapidly as the clouds were driven at pace over a blue sky by the wind, as if it were hurrying to drop them off somewhere. Now and then an overlooked pear fell into the grass with a muffled thud. The bees were sometimes carried a little way backwards by a strong gust of wind. Yes, she thought, maybe that's why. Maybe the funny feeling was because it was the first time since her childhood that she'd spent so long in a place she didn't immediately want to leave. She picked up a pear from the tall grass and looked at it. She'd never see pears the same way again. It was striped red and yellow, and Sally was trying to remember the name, although that didn't actually matter. There was a dent where it had hit, but otherwise it looked perfect. She bit slowly into it, let the juice run down her chin and recognised the taste at once. It was the same kind of pear that she'd fished out of the bowl of fruit that first morning. Suddenly she found herself grinning. OK, she thought, Liss is a witch with pears instead of gingerbread.

Liss. What was up with her? She took another bite then threw the pear away even though she'd felt like finishing it. Or maybe exactly because of that. Whatever. What was up with Liss?

'Hey, you, what are you doing there in that garden?'

Sally whirled round with a jump, and immediately felt annoyed at herself. There was no reason for alarm. She was entitled to be here. The shout had come from the school side. There was a middle-aged man standing there in a green knitted jacket that made him look kind of like a hunter. He had thin hair and a long face. Sally didn't like him.

'I'm allowed,' she said quickly and aggressively. 'This is Liss's garden.'

'Liss? Liss?' The man said her name in a disdainful way. 'Oh right. Why do you call her Liss? Who are you anyway?'

'What's it to you?' Sally retorted. 'Who are you for that matter?'

The man just stared at her for a while. Sally held his gaze. Her anger helped.

'I asked you,' he said, slowly and emphatically, as if she weren't quite all there, 'who you are and what you're doing in that garden.'

'Yes,' said Sally, 'you did. So just go fuck yourself.'

She walked out of the garden, trembling inwardly, not running. She heard the man yelling after her:

'Are you crazy? Are you crazy, you ... you little...'

Sally turned back, before she'd rounded the machine shed.

'Just say it,' she shouted back, daring him. 'Just you say it. Maybe it'll make you feel better. Bitch? Slut? Wasn't going to be "girl", was it?'

She headed back down to the farmyard, past the hens, who ran out of her way, clucking quietly, as if they could sense her mood.

Why was it like that? Why was there always someone to bring you down, to have a go at you? Why were you always surrounded by people who were as brainless as animals? More brainless, actually – at least the hens noticed. And why did she always react like that? Why wasn't she like Liss, who she'd yelled at too? She always stayed calm. Kept cool. Or if something fazed her, didn't show it, at least. That arsehole. What was it to him who was in the pear orchard? Did he think she wanted to nick something off him? Or set fire to something or something? Oh, no. She was just behind a fence in a garden where that idiot thought she didn't belong. Wasn't even his garden. It wasn't like she'd been in his shithole living room or anything. Furious, she picked up a piece of gravel and threw it at a chicken. She hadn't meant to, but the stone actually hit it. The hen staggered, cackled a loud protest and flew off. Shit. It was all the fault of that shitting arsehole who had nothing better to do than keeping watch over other people's gardens.

'Such underestimated creatures.' She heard Liss's voice float down, mildly amused. 'Did the hens attack you?'

Sally looked up. Liss was standing at the open bathroom window, wrapping a towel around her hair; she must have seen. Steam billowed out.

'Your neighbour seems to have a problem with me being in your garden. Had a go at me for no reason at all.'

Sally almost shouted it. She really wanted Liss to understand her, but all that came out was reproach and her anger that even here she couldn't be left in peace.

Liss said nothing. She vanished from the window for a moment, and when she returned, she'd chucked on a shirt and was casually buttoning it up. Sally had sat down on the wall along the old midden, which now housed nothing but planks and the wheelbarrows leaning against the wall. Still furious, she whacked her heels against the plaster. Liss leant out of the window and looked over at the hens.

'Nothing happened to it,' Sally shouted. 'It's fine. I didn't hit it hard.'

Liss twisted her lips a tiny bit. It was almost like she was smiling.

'The hen,' she said, 'is currently standing on a post, in a complete state, cackling to the other chickens: "Shit, ladies, you know what? That new girl is such a bitch. She just lobbed a stone at me. Hey, I didn't do a thing. She just threw stones at me."'

'What?' Sally didn't understand.

'That's all,' said Liss, shutting the bathroom window.

Than Sally twigged, and she jumped off the wall.

'That's not the same!' she screamed at the window, but then she found herself laughing as she imagined the hen telling the others about her. She didn't want to laugh, she wanted to be angry, but she couldn't help it.

Laughing angrily.

Fuck. What was the woman doing to her?

23/24 September

Sally had taken the transistor radio from the kitchen into the bathroom. It was standing on the wash basin and she was lying in the tub, singing along. It felt old-fashioned only to have a radio to play music on, not a phone: like something from another world. You couldn't choose what you wanted to listen to, just got what you were given, whether you liked it or not.

They'd spent half the day in the vineyard, after which they'd driven over to a meadow that Liss had never taken her to before, to pick apples. She hadn't realised how scattered the fields and meadows Liss owned actually were. She'd asked her about it. Why the fields weren't all together. Why she put up with driving several kilometres to get from one bit of land to another. And if she was rich. She had so much land. Liss had laughed and explained how things worked in the country. That you didn't buy all the fields in one go but, over the centuries, people bought one here and sold another there, married into one here and bequeathed another there. So why didn't they just swap them around between other farmers? Sally had asked, when they were sitting on the tractor and driving back, the trailer filled with sacks of apples. Liss had grimaced almost contemptuously and said that ownership meant more to most people in the village than logic. And was she rich? Sally could tell that the question had surprised Liss because she had to think about it a while. Yes, she'd said, eventually, slowly, if only the fields belonged to me and not to him. She'd been able to tell from the scorn in her voice that Liss had meant her father. But in any case, it was a strange way to be rich, seeing that she sometimes couldn't pay the bills. Land was also a load to bear.

Sally stretched out in the bath. She hadn't had a bath for ages. Only ever showered. But the unfamiliar ache in her back had worsened over the course of the day, the more apples she picked. She propped herself on the edge of the bath with her arms, and raised herself slowly into a bridge. Her head dipped under the water up to her ears, her body rose up out of it, shining and wet in the dim light of the bathroom lamp, and Sally caught her breath, almost scared, because she ... She dropped back into the water so hastily that it slopped over the edges. For a moment, she'd thought she looked beautiful. She shut her eyes to hold the image for a moment. The radio was playing a song she didn't know. Meaningless.

Meaningless. Was it? She opened her eyes again and looked into the clear water. She didn't like bubbles in the bath. She lay there in the water, tall though a little foreshortened by the refraction, but yes: somehow it looked beautiful and not meaningless. She was only now realising that that was how she'd seen her body most of the time. As if it were meaningless. The important things were will and strength. But right now, it felt good to be the way she was. Maybe that was because here she wasn't moving for the sake of moving. She didn't run for the sake of running. She didn't cycle for the sake of cycling. Here, she had to bend a thousand times to fill sacks full of potatoes or apples. Here, she had to ride the bike to get to the town or up to the vineyard or into the forest. It didn't feel ... empty to struggle here, to run up to the limits of her strength. She looked at the radio and started so violently that the water splashed over the edge. In the mirror, she could see Liss standing in the half-open door, looking at her.

'What?' she shouted, in a mingling of sudden rage and deep shock. 'What?'

All at once, she felt stupid and helpless in the bathtub, like a child, and she stood up and yelled at Liss, who'd withdrawn a little but was still standing in the doorway, a look on her face that Sally didn't understand and didn't want to understand either.

'What?' she yelled again. 'What's wrong with you? Are you...? Are you gay, or what?'

She was so angry now that the words gushed out of her. She felt so ... attacked, and she hit back as hard as she could.

'Why are you looking at me? What's going on? Want to lick me, yeah?'

She spread her legs obscenely, slipping as she did so, and she would have fallen if she hadn't managed to grab hold of the shower bar with one hand; that made her all the angrier.

'Do come in. Come in!' she roared after Liss, as she turned away without a word. 'You bitch!' she screamed, her voice breaking, helpless because it wasn't the right word, it didn't cut deeply enough.

She half fell out of the bath, wanting to get out of the water as fast as possible, caught herself with her hands on the slippery tiles, got up and slammed the door as hard as she could. Then she stood in the bathroom, breathing fast and began to shiver uncontrollably with rage and cold, feeling at the same time that the tears were starting. That made her angrier still. She had no reason to cry. That ... that woman! She couldn't make her cry. She'd ... she didn't know what it was that she'd done to her. She grabbed the radio and smashed it into the mirror. Although it cracked, it didn't fall, so she slammed her fist into the glass now. This time it shattered into the wash basin. Sally screamed as loudly as she could, took the radio, which was still playing, and hurled it onto the floor with all her might. She felt ... she didn't know ... dirty. Yes, wasn't that just perfect. She'd had a bath and got dirty at the same time. That bitch. That piece of shit! She'd ... she'd ... It was as if she'd ... when she'd trusted her. She'd fallen for it again. Stupid idiot. Stupid, stupid, stupid idiot!

She ... she screamed again, pulled a towel off the shelf, turned on all the taps and ran into her room.

•

She was sitting on the bed next to her packed rucksack, listening out for any sound in the house. At some point, she'd heard the woman go into the bathroom and sweep up the glass and mop the floor. Good. The bathroom had been under water. Very good. Then she'd waited some more until the reflection of every light in the house had vanished from the yard. She hadn't put a light on herself. She'd been sitting on the bed for hours, thinking nothing at all. She was just waiting. She never wanted to see her again, not even for the second in which she left.

She heard the church clock strike half past one. Everything was quiet. A thin moon hung in a gently veiled sky. She'd take the bike, she thought. That was the least she was owed.

Quietly, she stood up. Almost soundlessly, she slipped the rucksack on. She had her shoes in her hand. The cut from the mirror had stopped bleeding long ago, but there was still a large, dark stain on the bedsheet. With compliments, thought Sally, with compliments.

Quietly, she opened the door and walked noiselessly down the stairs, opened the kitchen door to get straight to the yard and saw the blazing red glow of the cigarette at the same moment that she noticed the smell. She resisted the impulse to immediately slam the door again and run away down the corridor to the back door. No. Then she didn't want it any other way. The woman was sitting there in the dark kitchen on a chair in front of the open French window like a sentry, and smoking as if nothing at all had happened. Sally took a tremulous breath and walked past her, ready to hit out at once if the woman touched her.

'No,' she said in a strained, quiet voice, once Sally was in the yard.

'No, what?' Sally shouted, not stopping. In the dark, she couldn't immediately find the latch on the barn door.

'No, I'm not gay.'

'Oh yeah?' Sally mocked. 'How d'you know? Never dared before, or what? Because it took someone that you thought couldn't get away, or what?'

She could feel the smooth wood now, and threw open the barn door. The bike always stood by the left-hand wall. She yanked it furiously over.

'I have tried it. I'm not gay. That's not why I was looking at you.'

The words came slowly, with an effort, half muffled by the night.

Sally didn't know what she felt. She was helpless with rage. She hurled the bike right across the yard, towards Liss. It skidded over the concrete with a clatter. The noise ripped into the dull quiet of the village.

'Why? Why did you do that? What are you ... are you sick or something? I trusted ... You just stood there and ogled me. Lusted after me. I saw it! D'you think I didn't see it?'

The cigarette lit up, illuminated Liss's face for a moment, and Sally could see that it was wet. So it should be.

'I'm...' Liss began, and paused. Sally didn't wait.

'Now! Say it. I'm getting out of here right now and if you want to say anything to me, say it now. I'm not in the mood to wait till you think of something.'

'OK,' said Liss, carefully stubbing out the cigarette. 'I don't care how this sounds, but this is how it was. I walked past the bathroom and saw you. When you ... you'd just kind of arched yourself up out of the water or something.'

Sally felt herself suddenly grow hot. Yes. That was the last way on earth you wanted to be seen. The very last.

'And? Turned you on, did it?'

'No,' answered Liss in a voice that Sally couldn't quite pin down. 'No, that wasn't it. It ... it reminded me.'

'Of what?' Sally asked harshly. She was still standing in the yard with the rucksack on her back.

Liss stood up. 'Of me,' she said. 'Of me when I was about your age.'

'Right,' mocked Sally. 'Yeah, right!'

'I don't know if it used to happen when I was that age,' said Liss, 'but these days, images from the past sometimes strike like lightning. They just hit you ... me. Full force. You don't know what that's like,' she added, and her voice got lost for a moment.

You could hear the quiet clinking of a chain from a barn somewhere nearby as one of the cows shifted. Otherwise, everything was quiet. There wasn't even a breeze to stir the leaves on the walnut tree in the yard.

'You don't know what it's like to stand in front of a mirror in the evening and look at yourself. Your breasts aren't what they used to be. There are blue veins on your ankles that you didn't notice yesterday, and there are stretch marks on your belly. And the whole time, there's the girl you used to be shining through this woman who's starting to fall to bits. The girl who used to lie in that same bathtub, in a house...'

Again she faltered. She reached for the tobacco pouch and Sally could hear, even if she couldn't see, that her hands must be trembling: she had to pull a second paper from the packet to roll her cigarette. She always made her cigarettes without filters, Sally thought, and it gave her such a weird, angry feeling that she knew these tiny details about this woman.

Liss lit the cigarette. You could make out her face again in the glow, but it was dry now and looked almost as calm as ever. Only the flame on the lighter was shaking.

'If I'd known, back then, when I lay in that bathtub at the age of fifteen, that thirty years later I'd still be … I'd be back living in this house … I'd have killed myself. So…'

'So, what?' asked Sally.

Liss smoked in silence. Sally waited.

'So that's why it is actually better if you go now.'

Sally didn't know what she was meant to think. She didn't know what she was feeling either, but she didn't want to allow her anger to die down.

'So that's it, right?' she asked, far too loudly. She wanted to break the silence in the village. She wanted people to be able to hear her. 'That's all? You only watched me because I remind you of you as a girl, right? That's so … I don't believe it.'

This time, a change ran through Liss. Sally could faintly see her stiffen.

'Sally,' she said firmly, and the realisation that Liss had never called her by name before caught Sally quite unawares, 'you have no idea. You have no clue how much you … the first time we met, you were angrily climbing the hill and it was like looking in a mirror with a thirty-year time lag. I can't change that. That's how it is.'

'Oh right,' said Sally. 'So you only let me live with you because I'm you. But a younger and prettier version.'

She said it to hurt.

'Maybe,' Liss answered slowly. 'Maybe that was part of it too.'

She paused and smoked.

'No. Actually, no. At any rate, that wasn't the main reason. I just remember how it feels. I remember how it feels at the point when you look at yourself and feel beautiful and special and different, to know that you were born for something more than this.'

Sally saw the red dot of the cigarette trace a scornful arc.

'And I know what it's like when that feeling, that certainty, of being special falls to pieces, a bit at a time, like a tree that's been planted in the wrong soil and forced, with stakes and ties, to grow away from the sun.'

She flicked the cigarette away. A tiny comet that sprayed sparks then dispersed on the concrete of the yard.

'I'm going to bed now,' said Liss in a very tired voice. 'Talked too much. Smoked too much.'

She walked into the kitchen. Barely more than a shadow in the night. But she left the door open. Sally stopped where she was standing. It was so quiet now that she could, very faintly, make out the chirping of the crickets in the garden. She jumped as half past two struck from the church tower. Two soft chimes. The kitchen door stood open. Sally felt the fury drain away like the water in a bathtub, and she felt empty. It wasn't until much later that she walked through the open door into the kitchen, shut it and climbed the stairs in the darkness. Her feet found the way by themselves.

26 September

Actually, the wordlessness was the worst part. They'd avoided each other. Liss had only realised that Sally hadn't gone when she'd heard the bathroom water pipes clanking. They'd then both waited until they could be certain of not seeing each other. Liss had breakfasted alone. Sally had breakfasted alone. They'd both been careful not to leave any trace of their presence for the other.

Why was the girl still here? Liss didn't know what was keeping her. But why was she still here herself? She couldn't have given a genuine answer, one that went any deeper than the flimsy reasons common sense could come up with: money, the hens, her work ... None of them were real reasons.

What was the girl to her? And what was she to Sally? Perhaps she just couldn't admit to herself that all she was doing was breathing through a mirror – overlaying the girl with a spurious childhood memory, sweet and enticing – through a glass that was only permeable in one direction. Could you really find fulfilment in another person? Let a girl who'd happened to wander by, and who might be stronger than you were yourself, live your life again for you? Live it better? She took a deep breath and drew herself up. Work. There was enough to do. She wasn't in the mood to follow that train of thought any further.

Sally wandered around the village. She'd taken the bike, but then not felt like riding away. It was unfair of the sun to be shining. It was unfair of the blowing wind to be lightening the day when she felt hard and heavy. She should have gone in the night. Or not. Actually yes. OK. Forget it.

But that wasn't so easy. The images were still there, inserting themselves – transparent yet unsettling – between the morning blue of the sky and herself; between the lorries that teetered through the village streets, laden with towering haybales, and herself; between the milk tanker and herself. And it was such a peaceful morning. The sounds were friendly. The hum of the tanker as it sucked the milk out of the barrels set out ready for it. The chugging of the tractors. Even the engines of the few cars out and about in the village. Nobody seemed to be in a hurry. Everything was simply taking its course, and the light promised the kind of afternoon when you could go swimming one more time, the last of the year. Except that there were these semi-transparent pictures of herself in the bath ... of Liss, who had looked at her. Of Liss in the yard, smoking. What did she actually want from the woman? Why was she still there?

Because there was no fucking alternative. Because everything else was much worse than being here. She braked abruptly and slipped off the saddle, the bike still between her legs.

Actually, that answered everything.

Because everything else was worse than being here. The thought struck home now with its full significance. Suddenly she had to laugh. Just to laugh. She knew that it was all only temporary. Even this laughter had really only been borrowed, this moment of liberation was only on credit, because she wouldn't be able to stay here forever, would she? But in that moment, it didn't matter. In that moment, the upsetting images had suddenly gone, as if someone had pulled away a grey filter that had been between her and the world, and she was seeing the village properly for the first time, in full colour.

'You don't often laugh, miss.'

If it hadn't been such an elderly, friendly voice, she'd have come right out with something mean, dirty. Miss! She turned her head. It was that very old lady, the one from the funeral; she was the kind you apparently only got here. In the city, they probably all lived in homes. She had never seen anyone who was so old yet so alive at the same time. Headscarf. Black dress, black apron over it. From a different time. Her knuckles, you saw at once, were as thick as burrs, swollen and a little crooked. Like a witch in a fairy tale. Except perhaps fairy-tale witches didn't ride bikes. That made her kind of ... it looked good. Such an old woman still riding a bicycle.

'No,' she answered, curt but not unfriendly, 'not often. But I am today.'

The old woman fished in the bag hanging off her handlebars and pulled out a bag from the bakery.

'Would you like a pretzel, miss? They always put an extra one in for me. I used to work there, you see.'

Sally hesitated. Anni held the bag out to her.

'Go on, you take it yourself. I haven't touched it, and it'd be a waste if I had to feed it to the hens. It's quite fresh.'

'I didn't mean that,' said Sally hastily. She didn't want the old woman to think she hadn't wanted to take the pretzel because she'd touched it first. 'Thank you.'

She bit into the pretzel. The crust cracked. It really was fresh.

Anni hesitated a moment, then said, in her thin, elderly voice: 'You're staying with Elisabeth. She's no bad person. You be kind to her.'

Then she climbed back onto the pedals, so slowly that she was on the verge of falling over, but it worked. Sally had a thought.

'Is there anywhere to go swimming around here? A lake or something?'

Anni stopped again. The smile she showed Sally had very few teeth.

'Now, in autumn? Mind, it's a very nice day today. Out that way in the forest,' she pointed eastward, 'there's a lake. I can't swim a stroke,' she concluded almost cheerfully, and rode away. Sally watched her. Then she leant her bike on the wall, laid her hands on the rough, sun-warmed stone and swung herself up. At the top, she pulled up her knees, put her arm around her legs and followed the old woman with her eyes as she and her bike gradually faded from view. How did the old lady even know her?

Be kind to Liss. Was that the kind of thing that old people just said, not meaning anything by it? Be kind to Liss. No. Liss was no bad person. Sally thoughtfully bit off a little of the pretzel. Inside it was still slightly warm. The salt on her upper lip was grainy and tasted good. She couldn't remember the last time anyone had made her a gift of something to eat. You only did that kind of thing with kids.

Liss was standing in the laundry room, sorting the washing, when she heard Sally call her.

'I'm here,' she called back.

When Sally opened the door, Liss didn't look up right away. She didn't know what she ought to say. She'd always found it hard to find her way out of silence. Sometimes she'd never even managed it.

'I had a swim. In the forest.'

Now she did look up. Sally looked cheerful. Like a perfectly ordinary girl, thought Liss with surprise, and something stirred within her, though she couldn't tell whether it was envy or joy.

'I've never been in here,' Sally remarked.

Liss saw the familiar room with new eyes for a second. It was here, and in the pantry, that least had changed. Apart from the washing machine, this room still looked as it had done fifty years ago. She only came in here when she had to.

'Does that burn wood?'

Sally had knelt down in front of the large laundry cauldron, which was set into the stone, and opened the furnace flap.

'I had baths in there as a child. Before we had the bathroom upstairs.'

Even to herself, her voice sounded papery.

Sally stood up, lifted the galvanised lid off the trough, let it drop again and grinned at Liss.

'I'll do that next time. Then you only have to lift the lid if you want to watch me having a bath.'

A wave of relief washed through Liss. Why, though? It was just ... no. It was no longer just the girl. It was Sally. Sally standing in front of her with wet hair and saying:

'You were going to show me that thing, weren't you? That steam tractor.'

'The traction engine.'

'Exactly.' Sally paused a moment. 'This old lady spoke to me. You know, the one who always says hello to you. She knew who I was. Anni, is it?'

Anni. Liss smiled slightly.

'That's OK. Come on. Time travel.'

It was cooler now. The sun was already low in the west, but it was pleasant in the light evening breeze as they walked off the street onto a large farm. The broad house was set back behind a chestnut tree – the tree had been old when she'd been little, thought Liss. Sometimes when she was out with Sally, she saw the village with different eyes. It smelt the same as ever, and it sounded the same as ever, and it looked the same as ever, but then it was as though … everything was a touch fresher.

'Doesn't anyone live there anymore?' Sally pointed to the dark windows. The tall grass between the cobbles said the same thing.

Liss shook her head. 'No, not for ten, fifteen years now. Not since old Heuberger went into the home. His sons are in the city. Nobody wants to farm these days.'

'What about you?'

Sally had stopped and was studying the heavy slate roof. It was a beautiful farm, actually. As a child, Liss had much preferred it to her father's.

'I didn't choose it,' she answered calmly. 'Come on. We'll go round the back.'

They took the narrow path between the house and the barn, which led into the garden and then up to the fields.

'Did they used to have to take all the horses and everything all the way around the village when they wanted to get to the fields?'

How rapidly and accurately the girl could sometimes think.

She opened the double doors behind the barn. The latch had rusted – she had to hit it free with a stone. Then she pulled on one of the doors. It scraped heavily over the uncut grass.

'Through the barn,' she said. 'Most of the barns are built like alleyways, so you can go directly from the farmyard to the fields.'

She pulled the other door too. The barn faced south-east. The traction engine stood as black as a large, lurking beast in the soft reddish light.

'Cool.'

Sally walked around the traction engine. Liss watched her as she ran her hands over the rough metal, opened the furnace door and looked inside.

'Can we heat it up?' she asked, but didn't wait for Liss to answer as she leapt in a single bound onto the iron step and then climbed onto the round body of the engine.

'You can fold out the smokestack,' Liss said from below.

Sally pulled on the reclining funnel and it rose up.

'Come up,' she laughed, 'come up!'

Liss took hold of the huge wheel over which the fanbelt had once run, and climbed up the spokes. Like the old days. Just as well she'd never been here with Sonny, she thought.

Sally had set up the chimney. It squeaked as it whacked into the bracket. The evening sun was in her face as she turned to Liss.

'Looks a bit like Thomas.'

'What?' Liss didn't understand.

Sally copied the face she was pulling and said: 'Thomas the Tank Engine, you know. And all his friends.'

'But they have big eyes and smiley faces,' said Liss drily, swinging down and reaching into the furnace. She came back up with a handful of soot, and before Sally had a chance to react, she'd drawn on her face. For a brief moment, Liss felt scared: too close, too much, but then Sally laughed. The soot was smudged over her face.

'And now,' she said solemnly, 'we need a top hat.'

Sally was surprised to find that it was getting properly dark as the two of them pushed the barn doors closed again. It hadn't seemed such a long time to her. Liss used the stone to whack the latch back into place.

'Shall we have something to eat?'

Sally nodded. She was really hungry. She hadn't had anything since the pretzel that morning.

The streetlamps in the village were flickering on, one after another, as they passed the church.

'You've still got soot round your mouth,' Liss smiled.

Sally stopped and rubbed her hands over her face. Then, just as she was about to follow Liss, she saw the police van and recognised her mother's car behind it, as they drove over the crossroads and onto Liss's farm. In a single panicked movement, she bolted away.

Shit! Shitshitshit. She didn't know if they'd seen her, but as she ran, she turned her head briefly and saw nobody running after her. She ran into the alley beside the church and didn't know where to go. Left over the fence went back to Liss's farm. Straight on took you past the orchard into the open fields. She'd be seen from miles off there. Besides, there was the poxy neighbour. OK. Where to? She yanked open the churchyard gate, ran to the door and tried the handle. Unlocked. She was so surprised when the door opened that she almost fell inside. In a church. Of all places. She nearly laughed, but then coughed because she was so out of breath, and suddenly her stomach heaved. Shit. What now? Her knees were soft and shaky, and she felt sick. She held on to a pew. Here in the church, it was almost completely dark. It smelt of old wood. Fuck. Why couldn't they just leave a person alone? What now? Just because they couldn't cope with other people not wanting to live in the same shitty world as they did. Because they wanted to pull everyone else into the same filth, the same stinking swamp, the swamp of broken aspirations and dreams and wishes and everything. And if someone manages to pull themselves out, along they come because they don't want to be alone in the rubbish. Because they want the other person's life to go to pieces too. Oh, rot in hell.

She looked around. During the funeral, she'd seen a door, at the front, by the altar. She went over and tried it. Also unlocked. A small room with a cupboard and a table, on which she could make out through the twilight a cross and a few cups. Chalices. They were called chalices.

'Sarah!'

Oh shit.

'Sarah. Sarah!'

That was her mother. She could hear her mother calling. Was she really that stupid? Sarah. She hadn't answered to that for years. It sounded like her mother was on the farm, or in the street.

There was another door in the little room, standing open and revealing a staircase. It went upward somewhere. Sally ran up it. Now nothing mattered anyway. It was even darker here than down there, and she could hardly see the steps. After two turns, she reached the pulpit, and there was more light. From there, you could see over the nave, but she climbed higher. The stairs seemed to go up the tower. She passed two window slits, through which she could see the roof of Liss's barn. Then she entered the tower room, where there was a glass case. In it, she could see the clock mechanism. And there was a ladder in the room. Right in the middle. Above it was the hatch to the belfry. The ticking clockwork was really loud.

'Sarah!'

Fuck off Sarah. Who are you, Sarah? Climb that ladder now, Sarah-pet.

When she was halfway up, she felt slightly dizzy. The ladder was pretty high. And going up wasn't the problem. Down was the problem. She shut her eyes for a moment. OK, she didn't want to go down anyway. Good job it was so dark she could hardly see anything. Keep climbing, Sarah-pet. Up, up!

It helped to make use of her mother's voice within her. It made her angry. Fortunately, there was a proper floor at the top that she could step onto. It was almost like an extra room, except that the bells hung here. And it was lighter here too. The sky wasn't yet completely dark, and the light of the streetlamps shone through the hatches. The floor was covered with pigeon mess and feathers, but there was a breeze coming through the louvres. She positioned herself on a cross beam of the bell supports from where she could see across the barn roof to a little of the yard and the house, but not the cars. She felt a little calmer inside. Obviously, she'd known she couldn't stay here forever. Suddenly she could see it all. In all the gory details. Her room. The kitchen where she ate breakfast alone every day. Or didn't. The way to school, that she had to walk every day. And everything else, that was now going to start again from the beginning. The nausea, caused by her race up here, welled back up within her, settled firmly in her throat and made it hard to swallow. She just didn't have the least desire to go back. She jumped as a pigeon fluttered up. Why the hell did everything keep making her jump?

Yes, why? What did it matter? It was over. No matter if she hid up here. She might as well go right back down. If not today, then tomorrow. Of course, she could go on somewhere else for a few days, but eventually they'd find her. And besides, she didn't want to go anywhere else. Fuck that.

The realisation hit her almost physically. For a moment she swayed on the beam and grabbed for something behind her to hold on to. It was the bell, and it only swayed very slightly with her weight. The metal was cool and rough. No. Hell, no. She didn't want to go anywhere else. The farm was the best place she'd ever been.

Over in the house, the lights went on. Everywhere. Apparently they were looking for her. She wondered how her parents knew she was here. Sometimes she saw a shadow pass a window. From up here, she could just see the kitchen, but Liss was nowhere in sight.

Suddenly there was a mechanical creak, then a rattle, and she looked up. Above her, a hammer was being drawn back; it was attached to a metal mount next to the upper bell. Then it clicked and the hammer sprang forward onto the bronze. It was unbelievably loud. She felt the sound through her whole body, more intense than any concert ever. Whoa! That was mental. The hammer moved back again and beat against the bell a second time. Again, it droned through the whole belfry, through her belly and her bones. Half past seven. She took a trembling breath. Then all at once she was calmer. It was as though the sound had forced the agitation out of her. She lifted herself up a little to get a better view. The house was dark again and now, first her mother's car and then the police van came into sight, onto the road in front of the farm, turned off at the crossroads onto the main road and vanished. Relief welled up in her, weakened her legs and her grip on the beams. She crouched down and shut her eyes. Oh, man. Thank you! Liss was awesome. She was properly awesome.

After leaving the church, she kept close to the barn wall, and then peeked around the corner into the yard, still trying to be quiet. Invisible. But there was only the tractor there, with the trailer. Sally ran to the patio door, but the kitchen was dark and the door was shut. Maybe Liss had gone to the henhouse. But the whole house was dark, and suddenly she had a bad feeling. A very bad feeling.

'Liss?' she called out. Quietly at first. Then louder. The front door was locked too. So Liss couldn't be in the house. There was no light on in the barn, and she wasn't in the garden either. Liss had gone with them. Or they'd taken her with them.

Great. She had no idea what that was supposed to mean. Why was Liss with them?

She walked to the stable door. Liss never locked that, and you could get into the house from the stable.

It was only once she was standing in her room that she switched on the light. Sally saw at a glance that her rucksack was gone. And her wallet. Now she didn't have a thing. No money, no ID – not that she could have produced it to show anyone anyway. She stood in her room and thought.

My room. Funny. Nothing here belongs to me. Still. My room.

She switched off the light and looked out onto the dark yard, without really taking anything in. If they'd taken Liss with them, they'd bring her back again. And then she'd either have to be here and let them take her home or back to the clinic, or she'd have to be gone. Why had they taken her rucksack away?

Sally needed money. At least a little bit.

It was the first time she'd been in Liss's bedroom, and it was totally unlike her expectations. There was a very large, self-built bed, completely surrounded by a huge mosquito net that hung from the ceiling. There was something a bit tentlike about it, especially with the bright, colourful bedspread, eastern-looking, from India or China. The bookshelves consisted of wine crates, but they weren't just stacked against the wall, they were stood on end and mounted on metal struts that ran from floor to ceiling all around the room.

Sally touched one of the crates, and jumped when it suddenly moved. Each crate could be swivelled independently. The room was full of books, but there were no pictures. Wait, there was one. It was hanging so that you could always have it in sight from the desk. Sally walked over to have a closer look and noticed for the first time that understanding a thing could make you smile, even if it was no smiling matter but a bitter truth. The signature told her that Liss hadn't painted it. But the artist was a woman, and that surprised her for a moment. The picture was vicious. It was vicious in a slyly funny way. A harlequin was kneeling submissively before a slim businessman with a modern skyscraper for a head, kissing his feet. Champagne was spilling contemptuously onto his back from a glass in the businessman's hand. There was a beautiful, half-naked woman dancing with a man who wore a deadly grin and a bizarre, colourful pointed hat. A crazed figure with very overlong fingers, a pointed nose and an upturned face was capering around behind them, screaming hopelessly at the sky. Winding between the dancing feet was a multi-coloured snake with a mocking face; it was skilfully binding the characters together while not getting trampled itself. Was that how Liss saw the world? The picture implied that the world was nothing but a poisoned illusion. That whatever anybody did, they were always thinking of themselves. Every transaction, every friendship, every love – whatever happened between humans, the snake was there. She couldn't help thinking back to the slowworm in the pear orchard.

But Liss wasn't like that at all. Or was she, and Sally just couldn't see it? Dazed, Sally sat down on the bed. Sometimes it was like that. You no longer knew a single thing. At that point, everything could be true and false at the same time. She noticed how tired her legs were, suddenly. She studied the picture for a long time. No. Yes. Actually, she kind of liked it because it was so uncompromisingly honest. Because it revealed the artist's opinion of people so remorselessly. But she still couldn't reconcile it with Liss. She'd never known anyone who didn't ... it was hard to describe ... who didn't take ownership of you. But without being indifferent to you. Someone who didn't want anything from you that you didn't choose to give.

She stood up again and walked over to the desk. If she found any money here, she could leave a note. Liss would probably understand. She opened the first drawer. It held nothing but letters. She was about to close it again when she noticed that none of them was addressed. She took them out. Thirty, forty envelopes. There must be three or four pages in each of them. Had she received them or written them? Sally looked over to the picture. This was not OK. She hesitated, had almost put the letters back, but she couldn't help it. She drew three folded pages out of the topmost envelope.

17 September

Peter, Dearest,

I realise I haven't written to you for a long time. Longer than normal at any rate. I should have done ages ago, but then there was always something that stopped me. A girl has arrived. Run away from a clinic. She is very thin, must be anorexic or something. But maybe it's something completely different – she is very tenacious. And a little bit crazy.

Sally took a deep breath. How strange it was to read about yourself. She looked at the letter again. The paper showed where Liss must have been interrupted: the rest was written in pencil not biro.

I feel guilty, Peter. I miss you so much. In all these years, there hasn't been a day, not a single day, when I haven't woken with the thought of you. But I don't even know what you look like now. I don't know how you think and laugh or cry – if you ever cry. If I'm perfectly honest – and I have to be, because you have to cut into the place where the wound is inflamed, you have to cut deeply there, until you get to the healthy flesh – I don't even know if I'd still recognise you. That's a scary thought.

But all the same, I feel guilty. For the first time in all these years, I woke up and thought not of you but of the girl. She reminds me of myself when I was that age. Except she's much stronger than me. And she experiences everything much more deeply. We went to the bees. She was stung and she almost enjoyed the pain. I have never seen anybody who absorbs everything like she does. Every image. Every flavour. Every sound. No wonder a person like that can't fit into a normal world.

I feel guilty because I'm starting to like her and because I know it's pointless. I've always lost everything I loved. No, that's not right: I've always destroyed everything I loved.

Peter. I miss you. I know I keep writing that, but it can't bore you – you'll never read it. But I miss you every single day. Until now. Now there's someone around that I have no history with. I should have sent her away a long time ago. But I should always have done the right thing, and I never did. And I'd so much like the experience, just for once, of letting someone go richer than when they came to me. Richer and healthier. Just for once not wrecking a thing that

The letter broke off mid-sentence. She turned the sheet over but the back was blank. There was another blank sheet too. Maybe Liss always wrote three pages. Sally folded the paper and put it back in the envelope, as carefully as if it were thin glass and might break at any moment. She had the same feeling as earlier in the bell tower, when the sound had reverberated through her body. Everything in and around her was vibrating at once.

Fuck. She shouldn't have read the letter. She didn't know what she was meant to feel. She shut the drawer and somehow didn't dare open another to keep looking for money. She accidentally brushed the mouse and the computer screen lit up. No password. OK. She definitely didn't want to read any more of Liss's private stuff, but at least she could quickly check her own email, and see if there was anything about her on social media, and maybe just what was going on with her parents right now.

She stood there and logged in, scrolled through hundreds of messages. It was unbelievable how much junk built up in a couple of weeks. She kept coming across ones from her parents, which she skimmed and which always said the same – they were worried about her and all that. And the constant plea to tell them where she was etc. The usual shit. The latest message was from ten minutes ago. Like ten more from her mother that same day:

> *Sarah, please get in touch urgently! We're so scared for you! We know you were on the farm. You mustn't stay there! That woman's a criminal. She was in jail for trying to kill her husband. Please get in touch if you're safe. Please! Mama.*

Sally read the message again. And then again. She closed the program, switched off the screen and walked out of the house.

27 September

It was all back. As if the whole intervening period had been wiped clean away. The moment she'd been led out of the police van into the building. No, not led. Invited, this time. But it was the same. Why did nothing in offices like this ever change? Even the smell of plastic was the same. And the insanely dry mouth was back, the weakness in her legs that she hated so much, the panic deep in her belly like an ugly, brutal dog that had just woken up and was about to slobber, bite, rampage its way up through her. It was after midnight now. She'd had to wait, been questioned briefly, had to wait again and was now in the interview room with the policeman and the parents.

'Since when has Sarah been with you?'

'I can't remember exactly. Early September, I think.'

'Why didn't you contact us?'

'Why should I have done? Is there a law against offering someone a room?'

There was a pause. The policeman looked at her. Sally's parents looked at her. They looked normal. Her father had looked normal too. They always looked normal. Did she look normal herself?

She tried to pull herself together. It was hard because her thoughts and her emotions were racing. She hadn't done anything wrong. Or had she?

'Where is Sarah?'

Sally's father leant over to her. He looked pale, and his breath smelt sweetish, as if he hadn't brushed his teeth today.

'I don't know.'

Sally's father was shouting now: 'So why have you got her

things in your house? How can you not know? You do know where she is. Where is she? Have you got her locked up?'

All at once he didn't look the least bit normal. Liss inhaled deeply and pressed her hands into her sides as if doing so could stabilise her. She wanted to shout in turn: what was he thinking, did he believe she'd killed her, or abused her, or hurt her in any way – but she held herself back. Of course he thought that. Of course. Everyone thought that.

'I don't know,' she said tautly, 'because she doesn't tell me where she goes. She was staying with me. That's all.'

The policeman looked disbelievingly at her.

'And of course you never asked her where she'd come from. Why a girl her age wasn't at school during termtime. Where her parents were.'

He wasn't asking questions. He was enumerating. Liss didn't know what she should answer. She saw that nobody there understood why you don't ask questions if you can see that you're not going to get answers.

'I don't know where Sarah is.' She finally forced the words over her lips. She'd have felt dirty saying Sally. 'She ran away when she saw you. She'll have gone on. Maybe she hid. What do I know?'

'You've done something to her,' the mother said quietly. 'Four weeks. Four weeks Sarah's with you and doesn't get in touch, and you claim not to have had a clue that she was ill, even though the girl's walked right out of a clinic. You ... you've done something to her.'

Liss felt the red rise up inside her. The dog inside her barked hoarsely.

'I gave the girl a bloody home,' she shouted, and jumped up and would have loved to have slapped them around the faces with it, but she just clenched her fists, trembling, seeing everything through the veil of rage. The mother stood up too.

'Who even are you? Her mother? You're ... just some random person. You're a criminal. You do not give my daughter a home! How can you ... Who do you think you are?'

Her voice had still been quiet, but full of hate, and the policeman raised his hands.

'Sit down, please. Both of you. Sit down! And calm down. We'll clear this up. We'll clear it up.'

Why did he always say everything twice? Liss sat down reluctantly, although the anger inside her was now much stronger than the fear. She only knew that she had done something right, something that everyone else called wrong. Just like before.

'I would like to go now.' She got the words out with an effort.

'Won't you just tell us where the girl is?' asked the policeman. 'Just take a look at her parents. If it were your child...'

That brought Liss to her feet.

'Don't you speak to me about that. Don't you dare!' she shouted, all self-control gone. 'I'm walking out of here now, and I don't give a shit whether you find Sally or not. I haven't hidden her. I did nothing more than give her a room, and if you want to hunt her, go ahead. You go ahead, find her and break her. You people are good at that kind of thing. Find her and break her!'

She tried to open the door, but it was locked. Obviously. It was a police station. She whirled around.

'Open it,' she hissed. 'Open it!'

The policeman pressed the buzzer, and Liss yanked the door open.

'You're surely not just letting her go?' the father asked incredulously. 'But she knows where our daughter is. You can't just...'

Liss didn't look back as she went down the stairs. Her whole body was trembling. She missed a step and almost fell.

As she left the station, she started to cry uncontrollably with rage, and she beat her fist against the rough plaster of the building, again and again, until it started to turn red.

30 September

The worst of it was what was missing. Sally had had no idea of how much she'd got used to in such a short time. Surfacing slowly from sleep, an occasional cockcrow or the gentle clucking of the hens coming through to her, always sounding so peaceful. Everyone assuring each other that everything was as it should be, time and time again. The soft tones of the bells chiming in the church tower across the barn. Although she now knew how powerful that sound could be, it had always sounded soft. On the farm, waking up hadn't been bad.

She sat at her desk and arranged things. Her phone precisely in the top right-hand corner. Her parents had brought it back from the clinic. She still hadn't charged it and switched it on. Her laptop parallel to the bottom edge of the desk. Ten centimetres. She took the ruler from her pen pot and measured it out. The new schoolbooks for her final year stacked in size order to the left of the laptop. Fifteen centimetres, she determined, and placed the ruler down. I could get a calendar too, and cross off the days. Days until exams and university and getting married and going nuts and kicking the bucket. Calendars with that many pages don't even exist.

She laughed quietly. I can always stick a few together.

Finally get your life in order.

Try to get to grips with reality for once, just for once.

That's simply how life is. Nothing is simple. You need structure.

Yeah. Thanks a bunch, Mama. Thanks a bunch, Papa; nice of you to have stayed here overnight for once, so that I could see you over breakfast when it wasn't even my birthday. I'll order my life now.

She laid her right hand on the desktop and used the black Edding marker pen to draw around the contours of her fingers. Now her hand would know where it belonged. She hurled the metal pen at the window with her full strength, hoping that it would break, but it just bounced back and hit her on the forehead. It was surprisingly painful.

'Sarah? Everything all right?'

Her mother's voice sounded wobbly.

Everything all right. Sure. Could she really be that thick? Did she really think everything was all right?

It was just that she hadn't known where else to go. And she hadn't managed to go on anywhere else. What would she have done there? There was only one place where she'd wanted to be. And she couldn't stay there anymore.

She looked out into the rain. It wasn't cold, but forlorn and gloomy. Thanks, weather. A bit of sad background music too, perhaps?

She hadn't been able to tell them anything. When she'd got home, Papa had still been there. It made her yearn to just run away again, right away.

What did you do why didn't you call we were so worried you could have oh God we were so scared scared scared worried why why why. None of them were real questions. It was dumping rubble. They knew where she'd been.

She dabbed black dots on her fingernails. School was the same as ever. The teachers all acted like she'd got cancer. Careful. Lots of pleases and thank-yous. If you need anything. If you ever don't quite feel. You can always. Why did they never finish their sentences? And people in her class were curious, but they barely spoke to her. If you want, you can copy from my book. I can give you the economics worksheets. We've started stochastics in maths.

That almost made her laugh. The subject matter. That had never been her problem. Her problem had been just not understanding how the others could be so slow. You just had to listen. You didn't have to do a thing. Just listen. She'd liked listening to Liss. Even when she wasn't saying anything. She'd liked watching her do things, all of which had a purpose. Picking up a hen to see why it was limping. Splitting a log to make a wedge to go under the sagging barn door. Or, right at the start, turning the tractor so that the drawbar on the trailer slipped perfectly into the coupler. Precision.

She propped her chin into her left hand. With her right hand, she used the marker to draw a frame around the display on her phone.

Most of all, she missed the smells. The pear mash in the wine cellar. The smell of the cows, which sometimes wafted up from the barns in the village towards evening. The smell of the potatoes that you dug up from the ground, and their smell once you'd boiled them and were eating them with salt. And the ancient smell of straw and hay in the barn, all sunlight and dust, when you sat on the floor in the open doorway in the afternoon, reading.

The woman tried to kill her husband. The words her father had repeated so often rang in her ears. The woman tried to kill her husband. She's dangerous.

Sally thought about the day she'd forgotten to write the letter. She thought about the deer they'd run over. She thought about the pistol that Liss kept in a metal case on the tractor. Then she snapped the cap carefully back onto the pen and let her head drop onto the desk.

1 October

Back then, in France, it had been summer. The ever-present buzzing of the cicadas was numbing, lulling, the sound of the south. Now, towards evening, a wind came up from the sea and blew away the heat that rose from the rocky ground, but it still smelt of wild thyme and bitter pine resin. The side door on the camper was open. She had used clips from preserving jars to attach a tarpaulin to the rail at the top of the van. With the addition of two tent poles, it created a large awning, almost a tent that could be put up anywhere, wherever they happened to be. She was proud of that little invention. Sonny had gone shopping in the town. The baby had fallen asleep, dressed only in a little vest, arms and legs stretched out wide, breathing peacefully on the sheepskin that normally lay on the driver's seat. Liss had laid her book down beside her and was studying her son. The sound of those words. Even now. My son. The emotion rising within her made her catch her breath: that sudden realisation that this was true happiness. Being far away. Being free, even if they had barely any money. When that was the case, they stayed where they were until they could fill up again, and then they drove on. Having a healthy child and being able to be there for him. Being able to read where she liked and what she liked and when she liked. Breathing this air and feeling this wind that didn't exist at home.

She stood up and took a few steps to the edge of the cliff. It was a little bay, and they'd parked the camper on the clifftop at one side. All the campsites were long closed. They could go no further south in France. When they'd first driven south, heading for Spain, she'd fallen in love with the landscapes of southern France. Spain had never been able to compete. The evening breeze stirred the light fabric on her body; it was almost as though she could feel it directly on her skin. The water in the bay had an unreal clarity. When she'd used to dream of beaches like that, she'd been unable to believe they really existed. No river, no lake in her childhood had ever been truly clear. The first time she'd seen such clear water, she'd stood for several minutes, just looking. And that fascination had never faded. If she swam out, she could see six, seven metres down to the seabed below her. It was still so incredible that this world existed. Her parents had never gone on holiday.

We're farmers, her father had said once. Who'll look after the livestock for us?

A ski trip in the mountains with the school. Two Protestant Youth camps, under canvas. And now here she was, in early October, standing on a French clifftop above a bay, wearing a summer dress that she didn't even need. She pulled it over her head with one quick movement and let it drop. It blew over to the camper and fluttered down like a weary, multi-coloured bird.

Wow!

Sonny had come up the narrow path.

You look good.

He put down the bags and reached for her. They did it standing up, breathlessly, hard and fast, and she had her eyes open, feeling Sonny, watching the sea and herself, as if from outside; standing naked, passionate, in front of Sonny, and for a moment she felt herself to be as beautiful as the water in the bay.

Later, they sat at the wobbly camping table and ate. Drank red wine that tasted so very different from the thin white plonk her father made. That could never taste good. After all, it wasn't made for flavour, it was made the way it always had been made.

We ought to think about heading home.

The words hit her like a casual slap in the face.

What? Head home?

It's nearly autumn. We've run out of money. And you have to ... we have to think about the baby.

For a moment, she was incapable of speech. It was such a long time since she'd had that feeling: the words gushing up in her, all wanting to get out, forming a traffic jam in her throat; sometimes she thought that must be what it felt like to suffocate.

We said we'd travel. We've only been away for five weeks.

Sonny had never taken criticism. Where other people felt caught out in a little everyday lie, apologised or tried to talk their way out of it, he went on the attack. She'd used to like that.

Do you think this can carry on forever?

He snarled now, sat upright in the borrowed camping chair, slammed the cup of wine down so hard that it slopped over.

Yes, I did actually think that. And that's what we agreed. That's why we're here!

The words began to find their way out. They were in a rush, sometimes she found herself stammering.

Think about the baby, should I? Me? Do you remember what happened when I told you I was pregnant? D'you remember?

That's in the past!

He almost screamed it.

Nothing's in the past. How can you sit there and tell me we should drive home because I ought to think about the baby? I thought about the baby when you ran away and fucked the first female to cross your path. Be glad you didn't get her up the duff too. Two years at least. That's what we said. Two years! I *am* thinking about the baby. I am. I don't want him to grow up like me or you. I want him to have a life, a real one.

With no money? In a camper?

He was mocking now, and that hit her harder than when he yelled, because she knew that tone so well.

Suddenly she felt dirty and vulnerable, half naked as she still was. She stood up and grabbed a T-shirt from the guy rope.

Yes. With no money. In a camper. But here. Or in Spain. Or Morocco. That's what we were planning, wasn't it?

The moon traced a silvery trail that bobbed uncertainly over the water, directly towards them. Over there lay Africa.

Your father offered to let me take over the farm if we get married.

She had to grab hold of the camper. At a stroke, everything was unreal, nothing was true. None of what she could see. The baby wheezed and curled up. She bent and covered his little body with her dress.

How long have you known that?

She could only whisper it.

Why does that matter?

He poured wine into his cup and drank hastily.

He'll retire for good in a couple of years, he said. He promised me. If we draw up a deed of conveyance, I'll have it written in. And then everything will be settled. You'll be provided for, and so will the baby. The farm is sound.

She didn't know how to move. She wanted to run and to sit down. She wanted to let herself fall. Sleep beside the baby till morning, then everything would be different. All of a sudden, she was dreadfully tired.

Don't you see what he's doing? Don't you see that he wants to chain us up like his dogs? A lifetime on a chain in his farm? In exchange for... She made a helpless gesture that took in the coast, the sea, the moon, the camper, the sleeping boy ...in exchange for all this?

It'll have to come to an end sooner or later.

He shouted it, grabbed the wine, stood up and walked off.

I'm drowning, she thought. I'm standing on dry land and drowning. The phrase ran through her head all night, back and forth, back and forth like a harrow, and in the morning her thoughts were nothing but a desert.

'Did you call the police and tell them the girl was staying with me?'

It was seven thirty a.m. She was standing in front of Gerhard, who was wearing only a sloppy T-shirt and Bermuda shorts, which she guessed he'd slept in too.

'What?' he asked sleepily. 'You rang the doorbell at this ungodly hour for that?'

'Did you call them?'

Her tone was so sharp that he woke up properly now.

'What? Yes! Of course.'

Liss stood on Gerhard's front doorstep and shivered. She'd shivered all night long, and only slept uneasily and superficially. In the end, she'd got up at five, sat in the kitchen and shivered there too.

'Of course? Gerhard, you're an arsehole.'

She turned and left.

'You don't get it, do you?' Gerhard yelled after her. 'You can't live like that. There are laws. There are rules. The rules apply to you too. People have to obey them! You can't just...'

He didn't finish the sentence. He probably didn't know himself what he'd been going to say. But it rang in her ears all the same. You can't live like that. Yes, she thought as she walked, yes. You can't live like that. It's like I'm invisible. I think I talk to people, and the words freeze in the air and nobody hears them. I should never have taken the girl in. The silence on the farm, now that she was gone, was almost unbearable.

She found it hard to work. Work had always been the thing she could cling to. But today, she found every step hard. As if the air were denser; almost like water. She felt an invisible resistance to everything she did. She didn't feel capable of anything. She sat in the kitchen and looked out onto the yard. The morning mist was starting to dissolve, and she could see that it was going to be a sunny day, and nothing stirred within her. She had always defended herself. Always. Time and again and time and again; and time and again they'd caught up with her, and now they'd managed it again. Her father. Her mother. Sonny. And then Sonny again. They'd all tried to diminish her. She'd always got up again. But what for?

Mechanically, she rolled herself a cigarette, and it occurred to her that it must be the sixth or seventh that morning already. Not a good sign.

There are only two places where they can't ban smoking, Beatrix had said once when they'd been out for yard exercise. One hour a day. In a yard where there wasn't even a tree in case you climbed it and got over the wall. As if that would have done any good. After the inner wall, there was another, and then the fence, and then one more wall...

Only two places. On the psychiatric ward and in prison.

Beatrix had seen both. She'd had that hoarse laugh that might be from smoking, though maybe her voice had always been like that. Because smoking is the only warmth left to you then.

But that's not true, thought Liss as she smoked and looked outside without anything stirring within her. It's not warming.

She went into the cellar, stood in the middle of the passageway and couldn't remember what she'd come down for. Actually, she ought to be able to smell the mash; the scent ought to be hanging sharp and clear in the air by now. And now it also occurred to her that when she'd been smoking just then, she hadn't been able to taste the tobacco flavour. Cigarettes always did smell better than they tasted, but she'd hardly been able to perceive anything. She hurried over to one of the mash tuns, lifted the lid and bent over it. Now the smell of pears and alcohol reached her, but still as if through a filter. She ought to start distilling, but the mere thought of setting up the equipment reared up in her face like a wall. What was wrong with her? Distilling had always given her pleasure, but now she couldn't even remember what that felt like.

She'd only been by the Atlantic once, but one image had seared its way deep inside her: in the evening, the landing stages were lying almost horizontal in the water. The waves broke hard against the quay wall, only a metre or so below the balustrade; you could feel the trembling of the stone in your feet if you stood still. It was a good feeling. But the next morning, when she'd gone down from the campsite to the water, alone because Sonny was still asleep and she'd got up because she'd been yearning for beauty, the sight took her completely unawares. The boats were gone. The jetties dropped away steeply and when she looked over the balustrade, she saw, about eight metres below her, nothing but a grey, oozy wasteland on which the boats lay around uselessly, tipped onto their sides. Five hundred metres away was the glittering ribbon of the waterway. She hadn't known what a tidal range was. She'd read about high and low tide, but the idea of the sea just flowing away, leaving a desert in its wake, had been beyond her imagination. She'd never seen the seabed naked before. It wasn't a pretty sight.

And that was how she felt inwardly now. As if everything had flowed out of her, leaving her as a wasteland of mud. With all the ugly and harsh and overgrown things that usually lay hidden beneath the glittering surface of the water now sticking out. All the things that sink to the floor within you, where they rot and fester. Everything had flowed out of her, and she was empty right down to the stinking sediment. She spun around on her heel in the wine cellar and thought: If I were a barrel, I'd throw me away. You can't put any more wine in there. You'll never get that one clean again.

She took two bottles of wine off the shelves at random, went up into the kitchen and started drinking, and she couldn't have said whether or not the wine tasted good. It was only a desperate attempt to pour something into the huge void inside her.

3 October

It was the first time in her life that Sally had been in an archive. You'd think that, in this internet age, you'd be able to find anything online, but the first time she'd searched for Liss's village plus the term 'attempted murder', the main thing she'd learnt was that everyone seemed to have tried to murder everyone else sometime or other. Shit, the internet was full of attempted murders. Pictures. Descriptions. Sick fantasies. Chatrooms. There was nothing at all about Liss's village. Not even a Wikipedia page. Or at least there was, but only about eight lines and a fuzzy picture of the church.

Eventually she'd thought of the newspaper. Sally remembered that Liss had learnt that they were looking for her from the newspaper. Probably a newspaper had reported on Liss at some point. She'd casually asked her parents, but they could only tell her what they'd heard from the police. They didn't even know when it had been. Helpful as ever.

The newspaper had a woeful internet presence. And there was no online archive for anything before the last three years. But she'd found out that they had a proper archive and that you could research as many articles as you liked there for fifteen euros. Every article from the last sixty years.

Liss's story just wouldn't let go of her. Shit, she'd lived with the woman for four weeks. They'd talked. Properly talked, not the way everyone else spoke to her. About real things. And they'd not spoken too. Most people just didn't grasp the idea that silence with another person was not only possible but the best thing of all. Because you could talk all kinds of shit with anyone, and it didn't mean a thing, but made people think you'd been God knows how close. Ben had always thought that. I love you. He'd really said that. It didn't mean a thing. They were just words. You couldn't sit in silence with Ben. Or her parents either. What's wrong? Something's wrong, isn't it? Why don't you say anything?

They didn't get that you were saying something the whole time. Just not with words.

Liss had understood that. She could do that. Sally couldn't get it into her head that she'd killed someone. Or nearly, at any rate.

Or then again, maybe she wouldn't actually have put it past her?

The deer. The way she'd shot the deer. Just as a matter of course. But that had been different. She hadn't *wanted* to kill it ... Shit. A thing like that probably happened just the same way. You didn't actually want to do it, but you had to.

That was actually worse: if you thought you had to do something like that because it was for the best.

Now she was sitting here. The room was dusky and looked almost like an attic. The walls were sloping, and all the windows were in the ceiling. You could only see sections of sky. But probably nobody needed much light here anyway.

There were machines that looked like ancient computers. But they were just screens that you could use to read microfilm. That sounded kind of good. Microfilm. It was like something out of an old movie.

She'd paid her fifteen euros, and some intern had explained to her how to put the microfilm in and how to view it. She'd asked Sally what she was looking for and tipped her off that you didn't have to read the whole paper every time – the police and court reports were always on two specific pages. Plus they only ever appeared on three set days a week, apparently. That made her search easier.

She'd looked at the last three years online. She guessed that the business couldn't have happened more than fifteen years ago. So that left only twelve years. Still a hundred and sixty issues a year though. A total of over two thousand pages to look through. It was going to be a long day.

Good job she hadn't gone to school.

Sally read through hundreds of brief reports on car accidents, thefts, blackmail attempts, punch-ups and break-ins. And hit-and-runs. Every now and then, a stabbing. There came a point when it was just flickering before her eyes and she had to lean back. Her back hurt. She was almost alone in the room. Only the intern was sitting at her desk, working quietly on her laptop. The screen was humming very quietly. She looked up. The window clipped out a very neat, perfectly rectangular, perfectly blue piece of autumn sky. Suddenly she was seized, almost physically, by a yearning to run over wide, empty fields and to see pears in the leaves, gleaming red and yellow against just such a blue sky. A yearning for the smells out there and a yearning for the freedom. Her legs twitched. She longed with all her might for what they claimed about Liss not to be true. Or for there to be another truth underlying what they all gave out as facts, polished smooth and conclusive – and yet wrong. She gave herself a shake and pushed in the next microfilm.

'You're pretty determined,' the intern remarked considerably later.

Sally jumped. She'd been so deep in her reading that she'd only taken in her surroundings as a quiet, constant static.

'Well yeah, I want to get this finished.'

The intern looked at her laptop.

'I hope you manage it. It's just that I have to close up here at five. You've only got another hour and a half. You haven't taken a break all day.'

It was a statement, not a question.

'I know,' said Sally. She could have done without the remark just then, but she didn't want to have a go at the intern. She was all right.

'I'm nearly done. Just eighteen months to go.'

The intern nodded.

Sally made an effort not to be distracted by how little time she had. In the worst case, she'd come back tomorrow. It was like a reward when she found the article she'd been looking for only an issue or two later.

'Husband Stabbed in Row' was the headline. '32-year-old woman refuses to answer allegations of attempted murder. Public prosecutor calls for 8 years.'

The sudden, electric surge of excitement after a long, exhausting day shot from her belly through her arms and legs. Hearing a vague story from her parents had been different from reading here what had happened. She skimmed through the article first, then she read it again slowly. She knew at once that it could only relate to Liss. An argument in the pantry had escalated, it said. The woman had grabbed a knife and tried to stab her husband to death. With a single blow. The public prosecutor had considered it an aggravating factor that Liss had known where to aim. She'd have been able to assume that that single blow would be lethal. That she hadn't wanted just to injure him. And when the judge had asked her if she'd intended to kill her husband, she'd just given her a long look.

Yes. Sally could imagine that. She was shivering inwardly, but her hands were still as she took the film out and carried it over to the intern. You could get a copy made.

'Found something?' the young woman asked as she took the film.

'Yes,' nodded Sally. 'Thanks,' she added, as if she hadn't been searching for the article by herself.

Sitting on the train, she read the article again and again. Being a court report, it held all the details but, in reality, it was just the starting point for the questions. Liss had said nothing in court. Why not? Had Sally missed the article on the outcome of the case? Had Liss actually got eight years? And how had the argument actually gone? The newspaper told her everything and nothing. Years of rows. Repeated physical assaults, a neighbour had testified. Who was that? The miserable old git from the pear orchard? But would Liss then ever have borrowed his van again? And why was she still living on the farm where everything seemed to have happened? She'd never have gone back herself, she thought. Back there.

Sally remembered the pantry, where she and Liss had made the bread. There? Then she thought about her room. Had the husband worked there? Slept there? Or with her?

It was still sunny. The train was running across a bit of countryside now. Not very far, and there were still houses somewhere in the background, but there was a lane there, lined with maple trees. Overall, they were still green, but where they faced south, there were the first patches of red glowing in the low-hanging sun.

She ought to be seeing that. She ought to be seeing that and finding it as beautiful as I do. She ought to be sitting beside me and seeing that because she was the one who enabled me even to notice that red.

It was strange to admit that to herself. Sally sat very still. The trees were long gone. The suburbs were creeping up to the railway line, ever nearer, and eventually enclosed it. The ugly brick-built backs of houses flew past. Like a prison, she thought, and then she tried to imagine sitting in a building like that for eight years. On the other side of the wall, only able to hear the trains.

For eight years.

Eight years of no red maples in autumn.

When she got off the train, she knew what she had to do.

4 October

You couldn't take the boy swimming in the river. So they'd gone to the lake in the forest, where they'd used to meet sometimes. In the old days, when Sonny had still been so different. Wild. Free. One of the guys who tore up the narrow village lanes on their motorbikes, over the pavements, through neighbours' barns, and sometimes even took the cramped passage through a cowshed if it was the quickest way from one street to another, and just laughed at the shouts of anger, because who could touch them?

She'd first smoked weed at the lake. How daring she'd felt back then. And how precisely she'd known, all of a sudden, that one day she'd leave. That she couldn't live here, and that Sonny and she would make it together.

They'd first had sex at the lake too. One August night. It had been hot but overcast, so Sonny had left the bike headlights on and shone them on the lake; if you were in the water and looked towards the bank, it shone like a moon that had slipped down between the trees. They swam naked. Before Sonny, she'd never dared. They swam naked and their legs touched, cool in the water, and it sent a shiver through her whole body each time. The muddy ground felt warm beneath their feet as they waded out of the lake. As she started drying herself with her T-shirt, he came over, took it out of her hand, chucked it away and kissed her. In the grass by the shore, in the moonlight from the bike headlamps, they'd made love.

She found herself thinking about that as she watched Sonny getting undressed. She always found herself thinking about it if they came to the lake, but that didn't happen very often now. Her son was sitting on the blanket she'd spread out, tangling himself in his shirt as he tried to pull it over his head without unbuttoning it. She had to laugh.

Come on, I'll help you.

No, I can do it.

His face got stuck in the shirt and as he tried to free himself, he fell over backwards and had to laugh too. She looked up to Sonny, but he wasn't laughing. He'd already been impatient on the way, taken the corners sharply, tailgated more than normal and had consequently had to keep braking hard.

She smiled up at him. Sometimes that still worked, but today he stood over them, his mouth not twitching. Querulous, thin-lipped:

A storm's coming and we want time to swim, don't we?

Liss looked to the west. There was indeed a dark band of cloud over the trees, but it was still sunny and hot, even if the sunlight seemed to be falling onto the almost-flat surface of the lake through a fine mist.

Come on, Peter, Papa's in a hurry.

She helped him with the shirt, but he insisted on undressing by himself, pulled on his swimming trunks and reached for Sonny's hand. Liss suddenly had a thick feeling in her throat, as if she wanted to cry, and on such a lovely day. But she had suddenly felt as though everything were speeding up, as if time were slipping away from her. Him standing there beside his father. Seven years old now, slim and so handsome. There was a lot of Sonny in him. Even if Sonny wasn't quite as slim as he used to be, he was still very good-looking. What a strange feeling, somewhere between happiness and farewell.

She got up off the blanket too. The midges danced crazily around her. Because of the impending storm. Rapidly, she stripped off her clothes.

You staying like that?

Sonny pointed at her breasts.

What?

Liss didn't understand. She'd got bikini bottoms on. She hadn't brought anything else.

Are you staying like that?

Sonny, there's no one here but us.

She knew that tone and that look, and it got on her nerves. He said nothing but walked to the water. Peter followed him. Her good mood had suddenly vanished. He was good at that. It used to be the other way around. Before, he'd swept people along, enthused them, his whims sparking, electrifying the others. It was like he couldn't bear it if other people didn't share his optimism, his unconcern, and so he wouldn't rest until everyone felt the same way. But it was just the same when he was in a bad mood too, grumpy, irritated for unfathomable reasons. Then he dragged everyone down to his level.

Cold!

Peter was standing up to his knees in the water, flinching when a little wave hit him.

Come off it!

Sonny splashed him.

No! Peter squealed. Don't.

Leave him.

What? The water's as warm as a bath. There's no need for such a fuss.

Sonny splashed him again. Peter was almost crying.

Splash back.

Liss splashed Sonny. Peter watched for a moment, then splashed him too.

Stop that. Peter, I'm warning you!

The boy was enjoying the game. He'd forgotten that he'd found the water cold just now. They were standing in the mud and he was using both hands to throw water at his father.

Peter!

Liss laughed. Peter bent and came up again with his hands full of dripping silt, and threw it at Sonny. Sonny took two steps through the water and hit out. Peter fell over. For a second, Liss stood stock still.

Are you mad? Are you mad? she screamed as she picked Peter up; he wasn't even crying, because he understood so little and he'd swallowed water; then he spat and coughed.

Are you sick? Are you ... What the hell was that?

I warned him.

Sonny stood there, cold and alien, and she was both bewildered and angrier than she'd ever been in her life.

You warned him? He's seven! He's a child!

He has to listen.

You really decked him.

The boy was crying properly now. The mark of Sonny's hand was starting to stand out red on his cheek. Liss felt such a rage rise up inside her that she could barely stand it. She stepped right up to Sonny.

You do not hit my child. Never again!

Sonny punched her in the mouth.

It was windy but not cold. Good for the wine, she thought automatically, the grapes will dry in time and not rot. The thought stopped her in her tracks. She was still thinking like that. Why didn't that stop? It had no meaning any longer. The grapes would rot on the vines anyway if nobody dared harvest them.

None of that is my concern any longer, she thought. It no longer means a thing. And the fact that she was thinking that way was just one more reason. Further proof that she was caught in a life that had been wrong from the start, and that she could never have escaped. She leant against the rough wood of the shed. As a child, Achilles had been the hero of Greek myth who'd fascinated her most. He was so angry, the way she always wanted to be, so strong and so deadly. And every time she got to the part where the arrow hit his heel and felled him, she'd found herself crying, every single time. That was the way she'd been feeling since they'd taken her back to the police. No, she corrected herself in the silence, that was the way she'd been feeling since the girl had been gone. As if they'd cut through her tendons. Then all strength was useless. Muscles were suddenly pointless because there was nothing to transmit their power to. Outwardly she was still strong, but that was no use now. She'd been felled.

She walked to the henhouse and opened it. The hens came out, cackling – they'd been shut in for almost two days. Liss watched them scatter across the yard and garden, agitatedly searching for food. Hens could still run around without a head. She'd seen that more than once, when her mother had slaughtered one. Another of those images. They couldn't feel anything without a head. But somehow, they could still run without falling over. Without seeing or hearing or feeling. A literally senseless existence. She looked up. The sky was swept blue, tattered clouds scudded eastwards. As a child, she'd secretly called days like this 'sailors' weather'. She'd felt like a sail whenever she'd crept out into the empty fields and spread out her arms and felt the wind trying to carry her away. And now? She looked up into the sky and felt nothing. Not even the yearning. Inwardly she was already dead.

She shunted the trailer of wood into the barn, uncoupled the tractor and parked it beside it. She walked through the yard and tidied all the equipment away. The broom into the old stables. The pitchfork into the barn. The wheelbarrow under the roof, tipped up so that no water would pool in it. She didn't know why she was doing that, because it was all meaningless. Finally, the yard was tidy, and she went into the house, walked up to her room, sat down at the desk and took a blank sheet from the drawer of letters.

Dear Peter, she began, *this is my final letter to you.*

5 October

'Hey, Sarah, aren't you meant to be in school?'

Great. Why wasn't he in school too? Sometimes she got the impression teachers never did any work. It was Brettschneider. Sitting there in his corduroy trousers – he probably had four pairs, each in a different shade of brown – on one of the shabby plastic chairs outside the station bakery; she'd bet that was a latte macchiato in his paper cup because he'd heard ten years ago that that was the in thing now. The instinct to tell some story kicked in. I'm ill or on the way to the doctor's or I don't feel well today or some other lie. But then she didn't want that. Actually, you should just say what was going on.

'I'm not going today.'

'What?'

It was clear to see that her answer had flummoxed Brettschneider.

'What do you mean, "I'm not going today"?'

'It's not that complicated.' Sally felt the heat rising, but she controlled herself. 'There isn't even a comma or anything. I'm not going today. Sometimes there are more important things than school.'

Brettschneider half stood up, and Sally's muscles tensed, but all he managed was a feeble: 'Be careful, Sarah, just be careful. Even the school's patience has limits.'

She set out to say something, but then it was as though she looked properly and fully at him all of a sudden. The man was more messed up inside than she'd ever been. And nothing would change that now.

So she said, 'I'm sorry,' and meant it honestly. He wasn't to know that she was referring to him and not her own misconduct. Brettschneider sat down again uncertainly, and she walked on, into the station. Her breath steamed in the cold air. Autumn really was here now.

As she sat on the train, she had time to think. Who had Liss written the letters to? Who was Peter? Her boyfriend? Maybe her husband? How sick would that be, to write letters to the man she'd almost killed? And why had she never sent the letters? Maybe Peter was dead, whoever he was. But that would be weird too. And anyway, she remembered, Liss had written that she didn't know what he looked like now or if she'd even recognise him. So he was probably still alive and she just hadn't seen him in ages. Her lover maybe. And then that might be a reason for her to have...

But none of that really mattered – only one thing was truly important. She had to talk to Liss.

Suddenly, the train was going too slowly for her. And it was a local one, stopping everywhere. As she looked out of the window, she wondered how long it would have taken her by bike. Six hours probably, or maybe eight. The landscape was gradually changing. Almost imperceptibly, the first vineyards rose out of the flat countryside. The mist had dissolved, and a harrowed field lay in the morning sunlight, looking freshly combed. In another, a thin line of cornstalks stood, presumably narrowly missed by the harvester. There was something forlorn about them, a row of tall, green plants, queuing up in the emptiness, as if waiting patiently for something that would never come. She didn't want that to happen to her. She didn't want that to happen to Liss. Thinking back on the weeks she'd spent with Liss, she realised for the first time how little she'd learnt about her. Of course. She'd only ever looked in on herself. Her impatience grew all the more. She jiggled her legs nervously. In the end she stood up and walked down the corridor to the doors, leant against the pleated plastic joining the carriages and suppressed the desire to look at her phone. How quickly you got used to it again. Sometimes it had felt so good to know nobody could contact her. That nobody knew where you were or what you were doing right then. A luxury. All the same – at that moment she wished she had Liss's number. Or had had it before. She'd wanted more than anything to phone her the next day, but she didn't have a number or an email address. She couldn't even remember whether there'd been a landline in the house. The train pulled in and even before it had come to a stop, she was pressing the button. It was the first time she'd been here at the station, and she had to look around to see where the buses went from. Impatiently she ran to the bus stop, impatiently she sat on the bus and followed the route map, stop after stop, and it wasn't until they'd turned off onto the long hill between the vineyards and she'd seen the tip of the church spire appear on the horizon against the bright October sky that the impatience turned to nervousness. She had no idea what Liss would think of her turning up again. Suddenly her head was filled with images of a furious Liss, yelling at her to get lost, you brought me nothing but trouble I never want to see you here again you're just like everyone else get lost get lost get lost. And then the other images: Liss in the bathroom with that funny look. Liss and the deer. Liss, who she'd sometimes spent ten minutes watching in silence at the kitchen table.

No. She wasn't dangerous. Or yes, OK, she was ... Was that a thing; could you completely lose it like that? Would she ever completely lose it herself and attack someone with a knife? It had just been that one time and ... shit. She was thinking in the wrong direction. Maybe Liss was insane in some quiet kind of way, and her parents had been right after all. Somehow, knowing a thing from a distance was completely different from now all at once being right up close. Great. Just the thoughts she needed. Especially at this moment: she was there.

It wasn't very far from the bus stop to the farm, but suddenly she was in no hurry at all. She walked slowly round the corner, and first there was the walnut tree outside the front door. All the leaves were still green. As if time had stood still here. She was unsure whether she should just walk up to the patio door as normal and go into the house. The front door was hardly ever used, but could she just ... just like that ... whatever. She walked across the yard. It was tidy. The barn door was shut. She found herself breathing faster, once or twice. Maybe she'd gone away. But then she tried the patio door and it was unlocked.

'Hello? Liss?'

She entered the kitchen and called out again.

'Liss?'

Something was funny. It was too quiet. The hens. She couldn't hear the hens. She walked through the whole house, but she already knew it was empty. Then she passed the pantry and ran down into the cellar. The intoxicating smell of pears hung in the air. It was as though it was passing right through her and filling her entire inner being, she liked it so much. The scent refilled her with peace. It was like coming home. Slowly she climbed the steps again. Maybe Liss was in the garden. She walked through the kitchen to the yard and down the path to the garden, past the henhouse. Shocked, she stopped. The hens and the cockerel were all dead. Standing by the low wooden door was a chopping block with the axe stuck into it. Beside that lay the heads in a little heap. And scattered across the coop and the path lay eight dead birds.

Shit. Shit. Something was messed up. Something wasn't right. Why had Liss ... Liss had liked the hens. When she'd thrown that stone at a chicken, Liss had ... Damn. Damn! Her head wouldn't think. She slapped her flat palm against her temples a couple of times, looked at the dead birds and tried to force herself to think. What was wrong? What had happened? Why had Liss killed the chickens? Suddenly, as if out of nowhere, a brutal fear nearly floored her.

'Liss!' she screamed through the garden. There was no answer. Sally wondered if she'd really looked in every room in the house. She ran back, all kinds of shitty images from films in her mind: people who'd hanged themselves in bathrooms, or from the living-room lamp. In a panic, she ripped doors open, looked in the bathroom and the toilet, and even went up into the loft for the first time – she'd never been there before. Liss was nowhere. She tried to persuade herself that Liss had just driven out to a field somewhere, but she didn't believe it. The sunlight fell through the tiles, a slanting bar on the dusty floorboards. She pushed up one of the attic windows, set it on the latch and pulled herself up on the frame, so that she could see out. The garden, the yard, the street – all empty.

Come on. Think. She forced herself to breathe calmly. She walked down the steps and passed Liss's bedroom. This time she didn't hesitate. She walked in and saw, lying on the desk, the letters she'd found in the drawer a few days earlier. They were lying there in a neat pile. The envelopes were all dated, and each was addressed: 'Peter'. Only the name, nothing else. The top one was twelve years old. She rifled through; the letters grew more recent, and the last one was from yesterday. She ripped it open.

Dear Peter, this is my final letter to you...

Shit. Oh shitshitshitshit! She read the whole letter, but it didn't say where or when or how. She didn't know what to do. With the letter in her hand, she ran down, through the kitchen and over the yard to the barn. The door was shut, but it opened. As ever, it was dusky inside and the smell of straw, dust and the jute of the potato sacks made the fear reach up with a hot hand, up through her lungs and press two fingers against her throat. The fear of losing all this forever. These smells and the barn and … and Liss.

The tractor was there. But the bike wasn't. The one she'd always ridden. The man's bike. On an impulse, she went over to the tractor, climbed onto the running board and pushed her hand under the seat. It was as though something fell away from her when she felt the metal case. It was still there! And at the same moment, the fingers squeezed again because even as she pulled it out, she could feel it. The box was far too light. The pistol was gone.

Where was she where was she where was she where was she? Her breathing was shallow and rapid and panicky. She stood there, holding the empty box in her hand, and tried to imagine where Liss had gone. She had no idea. Where do you go when you want to kill yourself? To the forest? A field? Where would she go if it were her? The images tumbled as if tipped off a shelf. The bridge down at the river. The ivy-covered tree on the playground before they moved. The high-rise roof she'd been on one night with Ben, where they'd kissed.

She took a deep breath. OK.

Somewhere beautiful. Somewhere meaningful. That's where she'd go if she wanted to kill herself. She had no idea which places were meaningful for Liss. But she'd gone by bicycle. Where could she get to by bike? Personally, she wouldn't mind riding a long way because, if she wouldn't have to get back, the distance wouldn't worry her. It could be thirty kilometres. Forty. Whatever. Wouldn't matter if you were exhausted. It'd be all over anyway.

She stood quietly and tried to think like Liss. It was no use. She didn't know a thing about her. Or did she? By the beehives maybe, but she wouldn't need the bike for that. Suddenly, two things occurred to her at once: the old motorbike over in the machine shed, behind the beehives. And the place that she knew for absolutely certain was significant to Liss.

She hadn't found a helmet and it had taken a long time to get the motorbike running, and even that had only been because she was too bloody stupid to open the fuel tap. Because you always thought that if a thing had been standing around for ages it must be broken. Because you didn't think of the obvious thing, just kept making it complicated.

The charnel house. Why hadn't she thought of that right away? The charnel house. Please please please let her have gone to the charnel house. Let her be there. No, don't let her be there. Let her still be on her way. Let me overtake her. Let her ... let her not be dead.

She didn't care that she was kind of praying. The thoughts were just screams. She wanted something, somebody, to be listening. Someone to make Liss not be dead. For things just for once not to be the way they always were.

She rode down the country lane that she'd taken the bike down that time, in the rain, when Liss had picked her up in the camper.

She squinted. The wind made her eyes water, but she rode as fast as she could. When she came to the crossroads in the valley, she paused. She'd forgotten if it was right or left. She'd genuinely forgotten whether the river had been on their right or their left. She shut her eyes a moment and tried to force the image back into her head. What had the road looked like that time, in the rain? She remembered having opened the window. Holding her face out into the rain. Where had the river been? Left? Right?

And then suddenly it was back. They'd turned right, up the hill. The river had been to the left. *Fuck*. How could she have forgotten that? She accelerated, the back wheel spun for a moment, she swerved across the main road, almost fell, swayed wildly to and fro and got the bike under control again. She didn't have a motorbike licence and had only ever ridden one on suburban streets, never done more than maybe thirty. She hoped nobody would stop her. A black Audi was driving alongside her. The driver was gesticulating wildly, kept pointing at his head because she didn't have a helmet. Fuck you. She wanted to stick her finger up at him, but she restrained herself. No trouble now. She just nodded and shrugged, as if to say that she'd simply forgotten the helmet.

It couldn't be so far now. Shit, she just had to make it without encountering the police. Or ... no ... maybe that wouldn't be such a bad thing. She could tell them she was on her way to stop someone ... well, what? Stop them killing themselves? Double shit. She didn't even know if Liss was really there. It was the only thing she could think of. The only thing that allowed her to be not standing on the farm waiting for everything to be over. She was riding with everything the bike had to give. Breathing was hard. Her hands were getting colder and colder. She was shivering with sheer nerves, and the wind wasn't helping. She had to pump every breath into her lungs, trembling with agitation, and she kept exhaling far too quickly. Where was that dump? Where had they turned off? When the town sign came into sight, she slowed, but she couldn't remember the name, maybe she hadn't even noticed it last time. The church. You ought to be able to see the church. It had been up on the hill. She was rolling pretty slowly now through the place, till she finally spotted the spire through the houses. She got to the old town, and now she recognised the square where they'd parked. She rattled over the cobbles and up the lane to the churchyard entrance. Shivering with cold and stress, she leapt off the bike, leant it against the wall, ran through the open gate and stopped, as if someone had punched her in the chest. The bicycle was there. She'd been right. There was her bike, lying in the grass, among the withered leaves. Liss was here. What now? Should she just call out? But that might be the very worst thing. Maybe that would push her over the edge because she didn't want anyone to ... Maybe she was already dead. How long had she been there? How long could she have...? Maybe she was just lying among the bones with her head in a sea of blood she'd seen that before in year six Oskar it'd been Oskar the clown messing around on the banisters three floors up only year six falling down the stairwell at the end of break right after the bell falling into the stairwell and his head smashed open like an egg in a sea of blood such a dark sea ... stop. Stop!

She forced herself to breathe. Very briefly, she dropped to her knees, rested her hands on the path, wet and cold with dew, and breathed. Then she stood up and walked towards the chapel, where Liss must be.

The iron gate was ajar. The only light fell into the passageway from outside. Sally took a few steps in.

'Liss?'

She said it very quietly. If Liss … if she was still alive, she didn't want to scare her. But there was no answer.

'Liss?'

Cautiously she took another few steps closer. She was now in the spot where the passageway into the crypt widened. The thousands of bones shone faintly. There was nobody there, but the walls jutted out so she couldn't see if Liss was further to the right or left, by the back wall.

'Liss?'

Nothing.

Eyes closed. Eyes open. Now. She walked into the room, stood in front of the bones and then turned around. Liss was sitting in the corner. Motionless.

'Go away.'

'Hello, Liss.'

She didn't know what else she could say.

'Go away,' Liss said again, dully. 'I don't want you to be there.'

'Liss.'

Sally still didn't know what she ought to say. Now she was cursing herself for her stupidity. She should have called the police. She had no idea what you should say or not say, do or not do. She should have thought.

Liss was sitting with her back against the wall with the pistol in her lap. Her hair was chaotic, and she looked wrecked, as if she hadn't slept for days. Probably hadn't.

'I can't leave now.'

'Doesn't matter either way,' Liss said tonelessly as she raised the pistol.

'No!' screamed Sally. 'No! No!'

She wanted to jump but slipped on the damp floor, fell heavily at Liss's feet, waiting, even as she fell, for the bang; and hit her head.

She groaned. The pain stabbed into her nose. Somehow, Liss still seemed to have functioning reflexes, apparently you always had them. Startled, she grabbed for her arm, too late to catch her, but still. And Sally grabbed for the gun, without thinking. She grabbed for the gun, got the barrel in her hand and pulled, still lying on the floor in front of Liss. Surprised, but still very fast, Liss held tight and tried to pull it away from Sally.

'I'm not letting go!' Sally screamed in desperate rage. 'Forget it. I'm not letting go of this fucking gun. Give it to me!'

Liss said nothing, but she wrestled her for the pistol. Sally had got her other hand free now and was gripping Liss's wrist.

'You...' she gasped between clenched teeth, 'you're not leaving. You're not pissing off now. Not like this.'

Liss let go of the pistol so suddenly that she fell backwards. Sally hugged the gun tight to herself.

'Shit,' she panted. 'Shit, what are you doing?'

Liss still said nothing. She was crouching with her back leaning against the wall, her hands over her face, and Sally could see that she was shaking. Her whole body was shaking, and although she couldn't hear a sound, Sally could see that Liss was crying. Trembling, she got up and stood there cluelessly for a while. Then she slipped the pistol into her jacket pocket, crouched down by Liss and laid both her hands on her shoulders.

Sally didn't know how long they stayed like that. Having touched Liss, she didn't dare take her hands away, as if that were keeping Liss alive. She couldn't say anything, not the usual platitudes. It's OK. Let it go. It's not so bad. She'd heard them all, always, and they weren't true. It was bad. It wasn't OK. And you could never, never just let go of a thing the way they wanted to insist you could.

Liss didn't move. Sally could only feel her breath on her hands. Her back began to ache. It was such a tiring position, and it was cold in the crypt. Liss took her hands from her face and looked at Sally.

'I don't need the pistol. There are plenty of other ways. Go away, Sally.'

Her voice sounded almost as though she hadn't been crying.

Sally took her hands off Liss's shoulders.

'Why?' she asked in bewilderment. 'Why?'

In the quiet of the ossuary, it sounded far too loud, almost like a shout.

'Because it's not worth it anymore,' Liss answered in a dead voice. 'Look at me. Look at me. I'm broken.'

A strange fury rose up in Sally. It came from the anxiety, the struggle and from something else that she couldn't have given a name. She stood up.

'You're broken?' she cried. She pointed at the bones behind her. 'They're broken. You're not. You're not broken. You...'

Words failed her. She didn't know how to reach Liss, but then she knelt right in front of her and whispered:

'Liss, Liss, Liss! You ... I thought I was broken. And then I came to you, and it didn't matter to you how messed up I was or whether I ate or not or what I'd done or ... No, wait. You did exactly the right thing. It did matter to you, but you left me alone. And eventually I noticed that it mattered to you. That you wanted me to ... me not to be messed up. But you never tried...'

She was searching for an image. Liss said nothing. She didn't look at her. She was a long way away. You could hear the muffled sound of the church clock outside. Half past eleven. A faint sunspot flickered on the dark wall of the passageway. The bones of a thousand dead souls lay there and waited. It was all the same to them whether or not they'd be joined by one more.

'It matters to me if you're dead or not,' said Sally, in a fury of despair, reaching for Liss's hands. They were ice-cold. 'It matters to me. If ... if a machine isn't working, you take it apart and take out the broken part and put it back together again. And that's what they kept trying with me. To take me apart and put me back together again. But people aren't machines. And if there's something broken inside them, then you sometimes just have to let it grow back together again, and you have to give them time for that. You did that. For me.'

Liss didn't raise her eyes as she answered.

'There's too much broken inside me. It can't grow back together.'

Sally didn't know what she should say, but then her head shot forward and her brow banged into the woman's. It hurt. Liss groaned and Sally hissed:

'Then ... then it'll just have to grow together crooked, and it'll always hurt a bit. But it's better for it to hurt than ... than to be like them.'

She didn't pull her forehead back. She pressed it against Liss's head. Liss couldn't get out of the way, the back of her head was against the wall.

'I'm not leaving here till you come with me. I'm not leaving here without you.'

Suddenly Liss pushed her violently away and stood up.

'How? How am I meant to live then?' she screamed. 'For what?'

Sally was lying on the floor. Again.

'Shit,' she swore. And then she screamed too.

'For me.'

6 October

The memory was sharp and clear, but it still felt unreal. Riding pillion on the motorbike through the blazing light of a glorious October morning. The smell of the chestnut leaves that whirled up in their faces on the road along the river. The engine vibrating beneath her. It had felt unreal, and she had observed herself as if through a thick pane of glass.

It was a foggy morning, and she was glad it was so quiet. She didn't know how long she had slept.

I'm still alive.

Sally had brought her home. She had made her tea. In the evening, she'd cooked pasta. Liss had let everything happen. Everything felt as alien as your cheek after an anaesthetic at the dentist's. Like touching somebody else. Except the numbness was in her whole body and especially in everything that she should really have been able to hear, taste, see. Everything had felt alien.

I'm still alive.

The fog was so thick that you could only see the outline of the barn. Even the church tower had gone, along with the rest of the village. Out on the road, a brake light shone out red, blurry as an old-fashioned lantern. When the anaesthetic started to wear off, hours later, it began with pins and needles. Deep inside. If you touched your cheek, you could still only feel it in your fingers. But deep inside it was already tingling. Liss stood completely still at the window and tried to feel whether anything was tingling anywhere. She couldn't tell. She didn't know whether her feelings were only numbed or long dead. She opened the window. The warm air streamed out of her room; the foggy air came in from below. Liss shut her eyes and felt the fine dampness settle on her lids.

*

The kitchen was full of smoke. Sally must have been trying to stoke up the fire. She'd also made tea, and set bread and butter on the table.

Liss went to the stove and opened the little door. The wood, which had previously only been smouldering, blazed up briefly, and a plume of smoke filled the room. Sally hadn't opened the damper. She looked up from her book.

'It's not burning properly.'

'You have to open the vent.'

Her voice sounded rough. As if she hadn't spoken for weeks.

'The fire needs a lot of air at first. Once it's glowing, you can shut the flap.'

Everything was uncertain. Liss could see that Sally didn't know what to say either. How should she? After what had happened yesterday ... how could they talk to each other? There was only the stove. And the weather. Trivialities, the kind of thing you say in hospital, sitting at the bedside of someone who's terminally ill, so as not to have to bear the silence that constantly screams 'Death'. Yet everything you say sounds wrong. Liss stood up from the stove, walked to the table and looked at Sally. The girl looked up at her. Liss wanted to say something but it was the same as ever. The words backed up in her throat somewhere, none of them wanted to let the others pass, so they all got stuck. Only one got through.

'Thanks.'

Sally pointed to the pot.

'I made tea. But I don't know if it ... I think it's come out too strong.'

Liss sat down at the table. Still uncertain, she poured herself a cup.

'Strong tea's no bad thing on a day like this.'

They both looked out through the patio door into the fog. You could only guess at the world out there. It was like being on a ship.

'I read a couple of your letters.'

Sally's voice sounded raw too.

'I wouldn't have ... that's what made me realise ... shit. I shouldn't have done it.'

Maybe it was as well that she was still numb, so that it felt like nothing more than a slight shock running through her body. But then ... Sally had seen her yesterday: what difference did it make?

'We ought to distil today,' she said after a while. 'It's the right day for it.'

Sally just nodded. Liss couldn't say what she was thinking. She watched Sally as she reached for the knife and cut two slices from the loaf. It was only then that she realised that there hadn't been any bread. Why would there be?

'Have you been shopping? What time is it?'

'Eleven,' said Sally drily. 'You slept way later than me, for a change. And yeah, sadly there's no cockerel to wake us now. Bread?'

For the first time in a long time, Liss felt her lips twitch, but Sally seemed to misinterpret that.

'Too soon?' she asked cautiously.

Liss shook her head and took the slice of bread. It was dark and smelt fresh and spiced. She didn't know exactly when she'd last eaten. But she had to put the bread straight back down again. The emptiness boomed within her like a large, cracked bell at the thought that had just caught her unawares.

'They'll come and fetch you back again.'

Sally shook her head, not looking up. 'Nobody can fetch me now. Yesterday was my birthday.'

It took Liss a second or two to understand. Then the relief came, and she could say: 'Yesterday? Happy birthday. Could've been a nicer day.'

Sally shrugged.

'Could've been worse. Somebody gave me a pistol. That's quite a thing.'

Liss said nothing, but as she took the first bite of bread and watched Sally, who was reading her book again and occasionally drinking a sip of tea, she felt the pins and needles start, very faintly, everywhere.

10 October

Those were very quiet days. They were both still moving cautiously. As if they'd walked a long way on a frozen lake, over ice that was now starting to crack and to creak if you trod too forcefully. Like after a day of heavy snowfall, when you can't be sure if you're still on the lake or if you're already on solid ground, because everything is equally white.

Quiet days on which they spoke about nothing important. On the first morning, she'd buried the chickens right at the back of the garden, because she didn't want Liss to see them in the yard. Liss didn't ask about them. And she'd hidden the pistol. She knew that it didn't actually matter, because if Liss wanted to try again, she'd find another way to kill herself. But she still couldn't help it.

'We'll make schnapps today.'

It was the first time Liss had actually wanted to do any work. It was probably, Sally thought, like when you got up after a long illness and didn't yet know how weak you were, whether your legs would carry you through the day or whether you'd get out of breath right away.

Liss didn't talk much. Well yeah. She never had talked much. But right now she was saying even less. Not that it mattered. Liss spoke through her movements. And Sally liked the fact that she understood Liss; that she understood without words what they had to do. She watched Liss carefully layer wood in the steam boiler so as to allow air through. It took a while to get her head around the maze of copper vats and pipes, but she was no idiot. And following the tubes, the arrangement of various containers, thinking about where that meant the evaporated alcohol would condense, how it would cool and eventually drip through, was satisfying. She liked the sharp, alcoholic aroma of the pear mash in the pressing room. It seemed like a very long time since they'd been in the pear orchard. She liked the subtle sheen of the copper still in the firelight when she opened the damper to stoke it up again. It looked so old-fashioned, yet considered and effective. Some things didn't need changing.

'What's that for?' she asked Liss, pointing at the copper ball that sat above the still.

'It's called the onion head,' answered Liss as she turned a small red wheel. The pointer on the pressure gauge above it was moving round to the right.

Sally wanted to put her hand on it, but not without checking how hot it was. It was bearable, and she ran her fingers over the copper. It was smooth, yet uniquely uneven; an almost supple structure of thousands of tiny dimples and waves. Liss watched her.

'The copper is triple-hammered,' she said. 'You have to thicken it like that to stop the fruit acids reacting with the metal, because that makes it rough on the inside and changes the taste.'

'Feels awesome. What about this?'

She rapped her knuckles on something that looked like a steam-engine chimney, except that it was closed at the top.

Liss gave an almost imperceptible smile, and Sally realised that it was the very first for days.

'You'll like the name. Dephlegmator.'

'What does it do? Make the schnapps a little less phlegmatic?'

She was genuinely amused by the idea of secretly changing the character of the spirits.

Liss pulled over the mash tun and began to scoop the mixture into the lower retort pot. Sally took the other plastic measure and joined in. She couldn't resist tasting the brown mash, and instantly winced. It tasted sour, alcoholic, fermented, and somehow only faintly of pear. It smelt a lot better than it tasted. Liss looked over at her.

'All the flavour has been in the scent for a long time,' she said. 'That's what we want to capture now.'

They filled the pot. When Liss closed the door, she pointed at the drum at the other end of the pipe from the onion head.

'The dephlegmator is a great invention,' she said slowly. 'When you boil the mash, the vapours rise up together – water and alcohol. But you only want the alcohol. The dephlegmator is set up so that it lets the vapour with the higher boiling point condense. That separates the steam from the alcohol. The water runs back into the mash. The alcohol stays as vapour and rises into the swan neck.'

She traced the path of the alcohol through the still with her long, powerful fingers.

'I like the names,' said Sally. 'Dephlegmator. Swan neck. Onion head. Sounds like something out of a sci-fi novel.'

Liss nodded in silence.

'How did it happen?'

It had just slipped out. She'd been sucking on the question for days. It was like old chewing gum in her mouth, so hard and tasteless that she'd involuntarily spat it out. Liss knew at once what she meant, Sally could see that. Her movements were jerkier, and quicker.

'You don't have to tell me,' Sally said hastily. 'Leave it. I don't have to know.'

'Yes you do.'

Liss's voice sounded rough and hard.

'I don't know how to explain a thing like that. It always comes across wrong. I couldn't tell them back then either.'

Damn. She shouldn't have asked. It was far too soon. She saw that Liss's hands were shaking as she turned the red dial again, and the temperature indicator dropped a tiny bit. It was quivering too.

'I ... we had a row. He ... It sounds so ridiculous. He used to hit our son. Sometimes not once in ages. Other times it was two or three times a week. And sometimes he hit me. And I know that ... that doesn't mean ... that you can't just ... that that's no reason...'

She stopped talking and looked at the still. It was starting to drip from the slender tap under the long cylinder into the glass beaker beneath. A sharp, biting smell of spirits was suddenly in the air.

'To kill someone? I don't know. Tell me.'

OK. She'd crossed the bridge now, asked directly. Now there was no going back, and now was the point when something would be decided between them. She didn't know exactly what it was, but that was how it felt. Liss bent over the glass jar.

'That's the foreshot,' she said drily. 'It's poisonous and you tip it away. That's why you must only heat up the retort slowly. So the poisonous alcohols vaporise first and don't spoil the spirits. That's how I am too,' she continued seamlessly. 'I've always burnt hot right away. With me you get everything in one fell swoop, and then there's the poison in everything I do and say. I can't explain it. It wasn't the fact that he hit me. That happened, and I hit back. Sometimes it was almost like he wanted that. But that wasn't the worst. The worst thing was that he imprisoned me.'

'What?'

Sally didn't understand right away, she was so shocked. Liss must have heard in her tone how horrified she was, and she made a dismissive hand movement. The glass jar clinked in its bracket.

'Not like that. He didn't lock me in the house. That would've been ... you can get free. You can run away. You can do something.

But it wasn't like that. He locked me up inwardly. Through the boy. Through the fact that I'd never got any proper qualifications because I got pregnant so young. Through my parents. They were always on his side.'

She took a long pause before she spat out the last sentence, bitter and hate-filled.

'Through the fact that I still believed I loved him. So stupid. So incredibly stupid!'

Sally listened. She just listened. There was nothing she ought to say. Nothing at all. Liss's voice grew calm, almost businesslike.

'And then there was a day when the boy spilt the milk. Nothing more. He hit him on the fingers. Not even hard, but with absolutely no emotion. I stood up and said: come here. Then, in the pantry, I said that he wasn't to touch us again, or I'd leave and take the boy.'

Liss stared at the still. Sally was very close to her now. She touched Liss on the shoulder. Only with her fingertips, very lightly.

'He just kind of laughed slightly and said that I wouldn't get very far with no money and no job and ... that either way, he wouldn't let me go. That the boy and I...'

She faltered again, and Sally felt the way she tried to make her voice firmer as she said:

'...that we belonged to him. And that it would never be any different. And that he could hit the boy whenever he considered it right. So I asked him what on earth had happened to our...'

She faltered for another moment, as if it were hard to find the words. But then her face hardened and she continued:

'... what had happened to our love? I asked him. Said there'd been something very special there once. And he just said, just like that, like someone ordering a loaf from the baker, that he'd never loved me anyway. Maybe he only said it because he knew that would hit me the hardest of all. And then he said, very coolly, that he'd only ever been interested in the farm. Today, I don't believe that that was even true, I think he just knew how to beat me without touching me. I took the knife off the wall and stabbed him in the chest. And yes,' said Liss, raising her head and looking at Sally. 'Yes. I wanted to kill him. I tried to hit his heart. I just botched it.'

There was a quiet hissing and gurgling coming from the copper pipes. The boiler was giving off warmth. A stronger, clearer stream now emerged from the tap. Fluently, Liss swapped the glass jar for a drum. Then she held a test tube under the tap. When it was three-quarters full, she stuck some kind of thermometer into it. Sally watched her in fascination. She always moved so fluidly. She would have snatched up the knife in exactly that way.

'What's that?'

She pointed at the thermometer thing that plunged into the pear spirit and then rose up again slightly.

'It measures the alcohol content. We're at seventy-four per cent right now.'

Sally leant over and sniffed. It was a very subtle scent, not nearly as strong as she'd expected. A scent like a wind-blown memory of the summery, blustery day in the pear garden.

'And then you spent eight years in prison.'

Sally still couldn't imagine what that meant. What that had meant for Liss, who had wanted to kill a man who'd imprisoned her.

Liss was astonished.

'You know all that? You know that and you ask me?'

Sally felt a spark of the anger that Liss sometimes had. It was a good sign. Something was still smouldering within her. She held her gaze.

'I read it. Just that. Not the other part. You didn't tell the court.'

'There was nothing to tell,' answered Liss after quite a while. 'Other people put up with much more without wanting to kill somebody. I tried to kill my husband. The father of my son. Everything else is insignificant.'

The glass cylinder was almost full. Liss quickly turned off the tap and emptied the cylinder into a bucket that was standing beside her on the wooden table. She checked the temperatures. She opened the door on the boiler. The warm glow of the embers shone on her beautiful, angular face. Sally swayed for a moment under a feeling that surged around her like a sudden wave on the sea.

'It's your son's bike, isn't it?'

Liss supported herself with both hands on the table and spoke facing away from her.

'He didn't let him visit me. At first, I didn't want him to either ... I was so ashamed. I ... How could I have looked at him? Told him ... Hi, son, I tried to kill your father. Sorry. Like that?'

She fell silent for a moment. Sally bent to pick up a piece of wood that had dropped on the floor in front of the steam boiler. The scent of pears was much stronger now.

'When I got out, I bought the bike. It was meant to be for him. When we saw each other again. I didn't want ... I didn't want to stand there empty-handed. But ... we never did see each other again. He wouldn't allow it, and they moved away. As soon as he got out of hospital, they moved away. I've never been there. And he's never ridden the bike.'

Sally thought it over.

'You never say the names. What's he called? What's your son's name?'

Liss turned to her in surprise.

'But I thought you'd known that for ages. You've read the letters. Peter. His name is Peter.'

The aroma changed suddenly, grew heavy, much sweeter and oily. Liss reached out hastily for the tap and closed it.

'The tail is coming,' she said drily. 'Rotgut. It smells good, but it can spoil the whole batch.'

Again she decanted the spirit, then she retrieved the glass jar and put it back, before opening the tap again.

'I've never told anyone that before,' she said quietly, 'never.'

Sally fetched the crate of empty schnapps bottles and put it on the wooden table.

'Good job I'm here then,' she said softly after a while.

Liss smiled for the first time in days.

14 October

'Sally!'

It took a while for her finally to surface from her sleep. She didn't know how often Liss had repeated her name.

'What? What's the time?'

'Half past two.' Liss was speaking very quietly, as if there were someone else in the room she didn't want to wake. 'It's time you were getting up. We're leaving in fifteen minutes.'

Sally rubbed her face with her hands.

'I'm awake. I'm awake.'

Liss made a slight noise; in the darkness it sounded as though there was a smile there too.

'There's hot coffee downstairs. And wrap up warm. It's cold.'

She walked out of the room, leaving the door open. The landing light was on. Sally sat up. She'd had colourful, vivid dreams, but now she couldn't remember exactly what they'd been. It was as though the images were waiting just around the street corner, ready to return once she'd fallen back to sleep. She was hovering between wakefulness and sleep, and felt like she was sinking. OK. She straightened up. Don't fall asleep. But it was still an effort to open her eyes.

The crush starts the day after tomorrow, Liss had said. It'll be a full moon and a clear night. The crush? Sally hadn't known what she'd meant. Picking the grapes, Liss had said. Harvesting. Sally found 'crush' a funny word used like that. It made her think of crowded stations, or fancying someone.

'The crush,' Sally whispered into the darkness, as she stood up. Harvesting sounded nicer, she thought.

She shivered as she dressed hastily. The warmth of the bed had dissipated immediately.

The kitchen was empty when she walked in, the patio door ajar. The tractor was already standing in the yard, engine running. Sally drank the coffee in great gulps. It was hot and bitter. On the kitchen table was a cloth bag of sandwiches. A metal Thermos flask. Hopefully there was tea in it. She took the bag, turned off the light and went into the yard to help Liss. It was like going on a journey. When you got up in the middle of the night. Excitement at experiencing something for the very first time. The goosebumps from cold mingled with tension because your body was tired but your mind was wide awake.

The moon hung bright and almost round, high up in the blackness. Stars over the rooftops. It was nice that the streetlamps weren't on all night here in the village. There was a warm smell of diesel, but her breath steamed in the air, and she couldn't quite imagine that she'd soon be cutting grapes without gloves. She climbed onto the tractor. They'd loaded the trailer yesterday. Liss hurried across the yard. She was carrying a heavy iron reel around which a steel cable was wrapped. Sally jumped down to help her.

'Forgot the winch.'

Liss was breathing fast. Sally had no idea what they needed the cable for, but she lent a hand. Together, they heaved it onto the trailer. Then they both climbed up and drove out of the yard.

She'd never been on an open vehicle at night before, unless you counted her bicycle. They drove a little way down the deserted country lane. The empty fields on either side had been harrowed and, in the moonlight, they looked freshly groomed and relaxed.

Midway through autumn. Midway through autumn, it felt like something new was beginning. Maybe it was. They were still harvesting here. The seed was already in the ground. Even when everything looked empty and picked and finished.

Liss steered the tractor into the vineyards. A lot had already been harvested.

'Why are we only picking now?'

She called out over the noise of the diesel and the equipment clashing, clanking and jolting together in the trailer. Still. They were kind of peaceful sounds. Like work. Almost a chord.

'Riesling,' Liss called back. 'Riesling is the last grape. It's always risky round here if you don't get enough sun in the autumn. But it's the best of all.'

Now they were driving through fruit trees that some wine-grower must have planted at the edge of his vineyard decades back. They were unkempt and had also already been harvested, but when she saw a single, forgotten pear in the branches, she stood up from her seat, kept her balance, stretched and broke it off as they passed. Liss glanced over to her as she bit into it. The pear was ice-cold, tasted fiercely bitter and sweet all at once. A fitting breakfast.

By the time they reached Liss's vineyard, there was already a small group of people standing there in thick jackets and woolly hats. As if it were winter. She nudged Liss, who saw her surprise.

'Did you think we could do this alone? It's a huge amount of work. Really huge. You always need helpers.'

She left the engine running as she jumped down from the driver's seat.

'Will you help pass the things down from the trailer?'

The grape pickers were all from the Czech Republic or Poland or somewhere. There was nobody from the village. They were quick and knew what to do. Three women, two men. Sally handed them the baskets and tubs, and heaved the huge sledge over the side of the trailer – not that she had any idea what it was for. Everyone was cheerful, and one of the women put out a hand to help her as she climbed out of the trailer. Someone else pressed a pair of grape shears and a bucket into her hand.

'I show you,' he said, introducing himself by pointing to his chest. 'Jan.'

Sally looked around for Liss, but she was busy at the front of the tractor, unwinding steel cable, which she hooked onto the sledge.

'Down there!' she called briefly to her. 'You two start down there. Take the sledge.'

'Sally,' she said to her companion, and then they descended through the vines towards the valley. Jan was pulling the sledge with two of the huge, empty plastic barrels, the ones she and Liss had loaded up yesterday. Now she also understood why there were oval-shaped holes in the top of the sledge. They held the barrels, which then stayed upright on the steep hillside.

As they descended, she kept slipping on the woodchips scattered between the rows of vines, until Jan nudged her and pointed at the wires around which they twined.

'Hold on.'

She was starting to feel warm. In the other rows, the helpers were already at the bottom. When they got to the foot of the hill, Jan took the small buckets from the sledge and handed her one. Then he turned away without a word and cut a bunch of grapes to show her. The dew glittered in the moonlight on the grey berries. Jan pointed the tip of the shears at some that had brown-black spots on them; others were dark, still others almost black.

'Yes,' he said of the grapes he was showing her, 'yes. Yes. No. Yes.'

Sally had to grin. That had surely been the shortest lesson in the history of the crush.

'OK.'

And then they started. At first it took her a while to figure out the best place to hold onto the bunch and how to go with the motion as you cut. Where to position the bucket – in front of you or behind? Where to look so as not to miss any grapes. Now and then, Jan, who was already several metres ahead of her, swapped to her side to show her a technique, or to stop her throwing away a bunch where she saw rotten grapes. He took it from her, picked off a berry and popped it into her mouth before she could fend him off. He threw the bunch into her bucket. She sucked on the cold grape and all at once her mouth was filled with an overwhelming, aromatic sweetness that didn't taste in the least like a wine grape; it was much more like muscat, and somehow also like honey and apples in the grass. Jan showed her again what that kind of berry looked like, but she didn't understand how he could distinguish them from the properly rotten ones just by the light of the moon. Fortunately, it didn't often arise. When she felt an ache in her back, she found herself thinking about the potatoes. How long ago that had been. At the thought, she gradually found her way into a rhythm. It was so quiet in the vineyard. Barely anyone spoke. You could hear the rustle of the vine leaves, the grapes falling into the bucket, footsteps, other people breathing. An almost magical atmosphere. The sky above her was black, the moon above her looked as though someone had punched a hole in the blackness. Every contour was sharply defined. She could even see her own shadow on the ground. It was like she was moving in a black-and-white film.

What I'm doing here is old. People have been doing this for thousands of years. Standing in a vineyard and cutting grapes. And now me.

Without Liss, she'd never have experienced this.

Grapes in her left hand. Cold, sweet weight. Cut. Inspect the grapes. Grapes in the bucket. Move on a metre. Push aside the leaves with a rustle. Frozen dew. Grapes in her left hand. Cut. Throw.

This is where we met.

She hadn't even seen the vineyard then. It had just been countryside. Meaningless. It hadn't been the same vineyard she was standing in now. This vineyard was real. It had become real over time. Maybe it had been all the points of contact with the earth. When had she ever had her hands in the soil before? Bees on her skin? When had she stood in a tree? Yes. Maybe that was it. That and Liss, who didn't even know how amazing she was. For a moment, she had to stand still. Because she couldn't catch her breath when she thought about the ossuary. As if it were only now that she understood what it would really have meant if Liss had killed herself there.

I want her to know what she's truly like. I want her to live. I want her to be able to feel the same happiness at being here. In this ice-cold morning in a vineyard.

'Look.'

Jan had pulled her sleeve to make her turn around. He pointed to the left. The sky was turning pink. Black and sharp, the silhouette of the town down by the river stood out against the delicate lightness in the east.

'Wow,' she whispered. 'Wow!'

When the earliest hint of brightness was in the sky, Jan called up for the first time. She had hooked up the second trailer and swept both out again, and then lined them with the tarpaulins. Now she started up the tractor and engaged the winch. The cable tensed. Drops of dew scattered off the whirring wire. Liss blew on her hands. It was cold. Until now, she'd done everything because she'd always done it that way. As if something were moving her from outside. As if she were hanging on wires like the vines, and without them, she'd collapse in on herself. And never be able to get up again. But when she saw the sledge running up the hill through the dawn with Sally standing on it, keeping both barrels balanced, Jan walking alongside, Sally pushing off strongly on the right or left, again and again, to keep the sledge on the track between the vines, laughing with excitement and the pleasure of riding a sledge uphill with no snow, Jan beside her catching the joy from her and smiling, correcting the course if Sally pushed too hard; when she saw that, it wasn't just pins and needles inside her anymore. It was as though things were no longer just bouncing off her skin. For the first time in a long time, an image found its way in. This picture of a laughing Sally on the sledge, travelling up the hill with two barrels full of grapes as the sun rose. All at once it was as though it hurt to breathe – with the sudden small joy of being able to feel something again.

The sledge was up, and she and Jan reached for the first barrel. They hoisted it over the side and emptied the grapes into the trailer.

'You're quick,' she said to Sally and Jan. Sally had turned in surprise and watched her for a moment. Liss knew why. She'd noticed it herself – her voice had sounded different. That touch lighter that you could really only feel yourself. Like when you'd cut your own hair. Nobody could sense that from outside. Only you could. But Sally had noticed all the same.

They emptied the second barrel into the trailer, set both back into the sledge. Sally grabbed it and was already on her way back down. Jan looked at Liss with a small, almost mocking smile, jerked his head in Sally's direction and gave her a wordless thumbs up before descending again himself. She watched him go, and then looked east, where the horizon was now starting to burn red while the last stars could still be seen above her. For a moment, she remembered the hot day when she'd first met the girl. Here, in the vineyard. How totally differently Sally had come up here just now. How had that happened? Perhaps it was like the harvest. You might do this and that in the vineyard, you cut and scattered and directed – but growth happened by itself. Still, after all these years, it was like a miracle that the vines blossomed, that the tiny flowers developed into berries and finally ripened into grapes. You couldn't do a thing about it. It just happened. It depended solely on the soil and the sun. Perhaps Sally had just been growing in the wrong place before.

From one moment to the next, the sun appeared on the horizon, and everything took on colour. The vine leaves shone red and yellow. Hanging over the river and the long-mown meadows was a fine fog. The brief shouts of the pickers rang out downhill. Liss could hear Sally laughing. Then – as suddenly as the sunrise – she was filled with her first real emotion in a very long time. It was a shattering yearning to have grown up in the right soil herself, and she couldn't stop the tears suddenly running down her face. But then the cable twitched again and Jan called up that the sledge was full.

It was about eight o'clock when they took the first break. Sally sat with Jan on the sledge. Liss had a big basket with sandwiches, fruit, flasks of coffee and tea, sausage, cheese, pretzels and croissants. When had she done all that? Had she even gone to bed?

Sally pressed her palms together. They were so sticky with grape juice that she could hardly pull them apart again. Liss saw.

'It'll be a good wine,' she remarked. 'If the juice is that sticky, the grapes are sweet. Good winemakers can tell the Oechsle rating just from how sticky the juice is.'

'What's that?' Sally asked, eating a pretzel. The air was still cold, but she'd got so warm that she'd taken her jacket off ages ago. The early sunlight made the fine hairs on her forearms shimmer gold.

'The must weight,' answered Liss, handing around the Thermos flasks. 'How sweet the must is. That determines what the wine'll be like.'

Everything smelt of grapes, mingled with a dry and slightly spicy, tart bitterness from the dried vine leaves. From under the sledge, a very fine mist rose where the sun was shining on the churned-up soil. That was the best smell. She knew it from the potato field, but here it was completely different. It was the dark scent of the earth in October, and Sally suddenly knew that she would always associate it with this radiant autumn day in the vineyard.

The others seemed to go way back. They were swapping jokes and chatting briefly, sometimes in Czech, sometimes in German, but she never had the feeling that anything was going over her head. She was just a grape picker like the rest. Jan hardly spoke at all, but he'd helped her all morning if she'd wanted to know something. Jan handed her the bag of pastries and poured tea into the cup they were all drinking from. Funny that you could feel so good among strangers.

'Why did we have to get up so early? It's going to be a gorgeous day.'

Liss was already packing the bags back into the basket.

'Because the grapes have to be cold.'

She reached into the trailer, pulled out a bunch of grapes and held it to Sally's cheek. It was almost as though it radiated cold.

'They mustn't ferment too quickly. Before sunrise, they're almost at freezing point, and later when we press them, the must will be cool enough. That's why we have to carry on again now. We'll eat properly later.'

Sally stood up, and she and Jan headed for a row further downhill. It was now properly foggy down in the valley, but even on the bottom edge of Liss's vineyard they were high above the fog. The sun lit it up like a lake. Only the church tower in the small town below emerged from it like a lighthouse.

She took the grape shears from her back pocket and started to cut. This was so different from anything else she'd ever done. Different from school. She sometimes got a good feeling, a sense of achievement, there too. But nothing was like this. Working and seeing something happen. The bucket filled. Then the barrel. Then the trailer. Sure, it was all very simple. But it still felt right. Right and good.

By the early afternoon, they'd finished. Every part of her ached, but that was OK. They'd loaded up the trailer one last time. Liss wanted to leave two rows. Ice wine, she'd said. Nothing more. Sally would ask for an explanation later. Now she was just glad the picking was over. They'd started at three a.m. Now it was three again. Twelve hours on the hill. And she was hot. It was now one of those beautiful afternoons she loved so much. The sky in that high, bright blue you only get in autumn. The air cool and clear, but full of light. The river, the town, the few leaves on the trees – everything was colour. At around noon, a light breeze had got up, and all at once she remembered a poem she'd learnt at school: the landscape was like ... 'like a verse in the Psalter'.

'Let's go,' cried Liss.

They had loaded the sledge, the barrels and buckets back onto the second trailer, and Sally climbed up to join Jan. Liss had already taken three or four trips back to the farm with the others. Sally couldn't wait to see what it looked like in the wine-pressing room now, what it was like to unload the grapes down the wooden chute, through the window into the cellar, what it was like to make wine. The tractor and trailer jerked. Jan offered her a cigarette; she shook her head. The smoke smelt wonderful in the blue air as they drove through the afternoon sun back into the village.

The evening had soon come. When Liss climbed up from the wine cellar, the pickers were long gone. She was so exhausted that she could hardly stay on her feet. She wondered how she'd managed it last year without help. Sally had helped with the gleaning, destemming, pressing and finally the cleaning. That was always the worst part, because the work was actually done, and the cleaning was like an extra task that you longed to put off till the next day. But they'd done it. Hosed out the trailer, washed the barrels, spread out the tarpaulins ... The day was done. A week ago, she hadn't believed she'd ever harvest again.

In the kitchen, Sally sat with her legs pulled up on the bench. The radio was playing. Something from her youth. Sally had laid two little chopping boards on the table and the remains of the pastries in a basket. There was butter and cheese amid autumn leaves that she must have brought with her, and a few bunches of grapes gleaming darkly on the old wood. She'd opened a bottle of last year's wine too.

'I've never tried your wine,' she said, pouring her a glass.

Liss had no idea when someone had last laid a table for her.

'Thank you.'

'No,' said Sally, putting the bottle down carefully and raising her glass. 'Thank *you*.'

Liss picked up her glass too, found herself responding to the toast. It felt funny. As if Sally were celebrating something, yet Liss didn't know what it was.

'Is this a belated birthday party or something?'

Sally took a sip of wine.

'Perhaps.'

Suddenly she laughed quietly.

'Sure. But not for me.'

Another song started. It took Liss a while to remember. 'Cantaloupe Island'. She'd once heard it in a bar in the south of France. All alone. With a book and a pastis under Perpignan's incredibly hot midday sun.

Sally stood up abruptly and turned up the radio.

'That's cool.'

'It's old,' said Liss, stretching out her legs.

Sally looked at Liss and grinned.

'You're old, but you're still cool.'

She started to move to the music. Liss looked at her. How could the girl still dance after a day like that. The slow, driving piano chords filled the kitchen and felt strange in the autumnal darkness; strange and yet so alluring. The trumpets struck up; so serene. She'd always wanted to be that serene, that floating...

Suddenly Sally was standing in front of her, reaching for her hand, pulling her up.

'No!' said Liss. 'I ... I can't.'

Sally didn't let go of her hand.

'Everyone can dance.'

As if the rhythm had been sleeping somewhere inside her and was now slowly waking, she allowed herself to sway, only very gently. When the song was over, she wanted to sit down again, but another was starting up, much quicker; one she didn't know. Sally had let go of her hand and was moving lightly and wildly. It was so absurd. The sleepless night and the long day of hard work behind her. The music in her kitchen. Sally, whom she was seeing dancing for the first time. OK, she thought, OK. She let the beat move her legs. She used to like dancing.

'Hey!' laughed Sally.

Liss danced. The song finished, they drank some wine and danced some more. The kitchen lamp reflected itself and their silhouettes in the dark windowpane. Every new song seemed to fit. Slow. Fast. Hard. Suddenly, Sally ran out of the kitchen.

'Wait!' she called. Liss kept moving. It was so long since she'd moved to music. A new song, something about dragonflies in the sun ... about feeling good.

Slow but full of power. She shut her eyes and let herself drift around the room with the words, like she'd done back then by the sea ... She heard Sally come back, but didn't open her eyes. Suddenly she felt something trickle down onto her head, opened her eyes and was shrouded in a cloud of white powder, could taste sweetness.

'What are you doing?'

Sally had the packet of icing sugar in her hand.

'Icing sugar. Because of the mites of the past. Dance. Move!'

It took her a moment to understand. Then it was as though she had to laugh, she felt so liberated; she took the packet from Sally and dusted her with sugar too.

The radio played and played and played.

15 October

The last properly sunny autumn day lay behind them. The train was running along the grey river. The trees were dripping with wet fog.

'Want to come?' Liss had asked that morning. 'I'm going to fetch the bike.'

She'd been a little startled at first. She hadn't quite known whether she wanted to go to the ossuary again. But perhaps Liss had wanted her to come. So she'd nodded. They'd loaded Liss's bike into the trailer and taken the tractor down to the station.

'You park it in the car park?' Sally had asked, nonplussed, when Liss had turned into the station square.

'I can hardly leave it on the road,' Liss had answered drily. 'Will you get a ticket?'

Standing at the pay-and-display machine, she thought the tractor looked kind of awesome amid all the family cars. And she wondered where Liss would stick the ticket. The tractor didn't have a windscreen.

'Why didn't we take the motorbike?' she asked, once they'd heaved the bicycle onto the train and found seats.

Liss looked out of the window.

'I thought it might be nice to go for a ride together again.'

'Aren't you scared?' Sally asked after a while. A solitary barge drifted past on the water. Liss shrugged her shoulders.

'Sure. But not so much that I'd rather abandon the bike there.'

Sally had to smile.

It didn't take half as long by train as it had seemed that time on the motorbike. Liss didn't talk much, and she wouldn't want to talk much either. But it wasn't a heavy silence.

The station lay outside the old town gates, right in the industrial area. Sally hadn't often seen a town that had two such extremes: so ugly and so pretty.

Liss carried her bike up the underpass steps then they headed through the town gate and up steep, winding cobbled streets. Liss was still not talking. But as they crossed the marketplace, Liss pointed to a café they'd been to before and said:

'We can have a coffee before we ride back.'

Sally just shook her head, but she was relieved. There would be a 'later'. Stupid thought, but it'd been there. It wasn't to do with the place, but the people who were shaped by the place. And the Liss pushing her bike beside her was no longer the Liss she'd found in the ossuary.

'I hope it's still there,' she said, for something to say.

Liss suddenly stopped and turned to her.

'I danced yesterday,' she said calmly, and then a miniscule smile played around her lips. 'There's still sugar in my hair. I'm not killing myself today. We're just retrieving a bike.'

'OK,' she answered. She suddenly felt very much lighter. They climbed the three steps up to the churchyard. The bike was still there. Some kind soul had leant it up against the wall.

'An orderly country,' remarked Liss in such an ironic tone that Sally had to laugh. 'Come on.'

To her surprise, Liss didn't turned downhill, but kept pushing on up.

'We can ride along the ridge,' she explained briefly.

There was a small, very steep road leading up through a gap in the church wall, becoming a forest path almost immediately.

'I'm just asking,' said Sally, 'but are we going to walk all the way back?'

'Still feeling the wine harvest?' Liss retorted, smiling wickedly.

Wow. OK. That was the real Liss. Sally had to smile too, but looked at the ground so that Liss wouldn't see.

'Here,' said Liss, as the little copse opened out again. She laid her bicycle in the dry leaves at the side of the path. Sally just stared. They were standing in front of a ruined castle, which had simply appeared out of nowhere. Three storeys of empty windows. A massive hall without a roof. Steps that soared into nothing. Liss walked into the castle as if she knew exactly where she wanted to go, climbed the steps to what had once been the second floor, where a broad ledge ran along the wall, leading to the largest arched window. There were no railings anywhere. And although the ledge was wide, it suddenly felt much narrower when you walked on it. She was glad when she caught up with Liss by the window.

'Look,' said Liss.

Sally looked. It was a grey autumn day, but the view was stunning. It was as though you could see across the whole country. The river was a never-ending ribbon that at some point just melted into the horizon. Towns and villages lay scattered between the vineyards, which went on forever. Right in the distance, to the north, rose a row of mountains, a shade darker than the mist. It was a picture like still water; as if you were quenching a thirst that you hadn't previously noticed.

'What a beautiful landscape,' Sally said, sometime later.

Liss inclined her head ever so slightly in agreement.

Later, they rolled along the country road on the hilltop, through little villages and past harvested orchards. There was a fine drizzle now and then, they had a tailwind and cycling was easy. Things are in balance, she thought.

Liss caught up and rode beside her. Calmly, she said:

'I think you should go home.'

Sally turned to her, ripped right out of what she'd been feeling, stiffened for the anger that would boil up, and was surprised when it didn't come.

'You're welcome to stay. But I think that you shouldn't … make the mistake I made. You're … I think you're very intelligent.'

Sally rode beside her in silence. She didn't know exactly what she felt.

'You didn't let me run away,' Liss said eventually, with an effort. 'I want … I can't let you run away either.'

'But I don't want to…' Sally began, but then she understood what Liss meant.

'I should go back?'

Liss thought for a while, as she rode by her side. The road was starting to descend into the town.

'You should come to me whenever you like. But I think you should finish school. It sounds stuffy and boring, but it would be a mistake not to. And besides…'

'What?' Her insides were tangling.

Liss suddenly braked and stood up.

'Besides, I know what it feels like to lose your child!'

Liss almost shouted it, realised and lowered her voice.

'Put that right. You can't leave like that. Or you shouldn't. Even if they … I don't know what they're like. I only saw them once, and then I just argued with them. But somehow or other, they love you all the same.'

Sally took a breath. She wanted to say a thousand things. Explain to Liss that she'd got it wrong. That she hadn't a clue. That…

'Be sensible, right?'

Liss shook her head wildly.

'You don't understand! I want you to be able to come anytime. But I don't want you to stay because you have to stay. Look at me. Don't you get it? I had to stay. But I don't want it to be like that for you. I want the exact opposite – for you to be able to keep the freedom you have. You've ... you're incredibly strong. That's what you have to keep. You're strong enough to go home to your parents. To finish school. To decide for yourself when you come to me and when it's time to go. Get that? Who's going to tell you but me? Who are you going to believe it from but me?'

Liss was breathing very fast now, and Sally stood very quietly. She didn't like it. She didn't like it, but it was true. She laid her bike on the road and went over to Liss. She didn't avoid her eyes.

'OK. I'll go back. But you give me the letters.'

'What?'

'You give me the letters. If I go back to my parents, you give me the letters for Peter.'

Liss's face lost all expression.

'No.'

Sally couldn't help it, she screamed.

'Yes! We're both going the same way now. Both of us. I didn't take the fucking gun off you so you could carry on living like before. Here!'

She pressed their foreheads together.

'We're alive. We're warm. We're alive. Give me the letters! If it doesn't work, it doesn't work. But you're not even giving him the chance to love you. Give me the letters or I won't leave.'

She'd put her arms round Liss; brow to brow they stood there in the middle of the country lane, like a strange pair of lovers, filled with rage and love, as Sally breathed wildly and never stopped pressing her forehead against Liss's, as if she could transmit her thoughts to her too.

Very slowly, Liss softened in Sally's grasp. Her muscles relaxed.

'Fine,' she mumbled, almost inaudibly.

'No,' Sally demanded, 'you have to want it. Do you want it? Do you really?'

'Yes!' yelled Liss, tearing herself free furiously. 'Yes. Of course. You get the letters. And now let's go.'

She grabbed up her bike and rode away, as fast as she could. But Sally wouldn't be shaken off. They were both pedalling as hard as they could. They were neck and neck, and Sally rode the anger and jitters and a dash of fear out of her body as the road grew ever steeper and they plunged towards the town.

'Faster!' she screamed to Liss. 'Ride faster.'

The wind roared around their ears and their jackets fluttered as they raced side by side, took the corners together, and finally passed the town sign, behind which a sad smiley lit up, announcing affrontedly, in red digital letters: *Your speed: 42 kph. Please slow down!*

Then she heard Liss laugh, and then she could brake.

They were sitting on the tractor, driving through the early dusk. The village appeared on the horizon. A few windows here and there were already lit up. They'd been sweating and now it was getting chilly.

'What will you do with the letters?' asked Liss.

'Burn them,' said Sally. She had to laugh when she saw Liss's face. 'No. I'll send them to him. One at a time. He has to get to know you again before he sees you.'

Liss took her foot off the accelerator. They turned onto the track that was a shortcut to the farm.

'Maybe he won't want to see me.'

'Maybe he won't,' said Sally. 'But maybe he will. Why shouldn't he? You're an amazing woman.'

They fell silent. Sally stretched out her hand as they passed the bare hazel bushes. Liss saw it and it was as though she could feel the dewdrops and the rough bark in her own palms.

'Once I've done my shitting exams,' Sally said, 'we'll go to the Med.'

Liss didn't answer until they turned into the farm.

'I'll pick you up,' she said, lifting the wheels of the trailer.

'You haven't got a car.'

Liss pointed at the trailer.

'You can't see it yet, but one day that'll be a caravan. On the day you get your results, I'll be standing outside your school.'

'With the tractor?'

Sally had to laugh at the idea. Liss smiled and shrugged.

'You said it. I haven't got a car.'

They were standing in the yard. The streetlamps were coming on. The church clock struck quarter to. The fallen leaves under the tree by the front door gave off a strong smell of walnuts. Coming very slowly round the corner was a rickety bicycle. Anni was riding to the church to do the flowers. When she saw the two of them, she stopped.

'You two will look after each other, yes!' she said in her brittle, elderly voice, and it wasn't a question.

'Yes,' said Sally.

'Yes,' said Liss.

Anni climbed off, leant the bike thoughtfully against the fence, bent and picked up a walnut.

'Like I said,' she remarked with satisfaction, as if to herself, getting back on her bike, 'a lovely autumn.'

ACKNOWLEDGEMENTS

No book writes itself. A bestseller is not worked out at the desk and it is not the author who does it. It is all of you! So please let me thank *you*:

- Annette Weber, for all the talks at weird times and places, who made this text a real book.
- Sabine Cramer and Karen Sullivan, my German and British editors, for their courage to take a non-love story into their programme.
- Rachel Ward, who did an awesome job trans-*lating* this text onto another level. Rachel, I never read any of my books again, but with your recreation of the text I could not only do it without blushing with shame, but was even able to read it as a new work.
- My always-present team at Orenda, any of whom would answer a mail at virtually any time. You paved *Sunlight*'s path to the English-speaking world!
- All you booksellers out there. A bestseller is not the book piled in the stores. It is the book sold by you – and this is a tough job these days. Thank you for reading, recommending, giving feedback and advice, and, of course, for selling ;-)
- Finally my family; especially Viktoria, who added a great deal to this book.